# No One Survives

## Rotten: Book 2

**Buzz Parcher**

# Contents

# PREFACE

If you or anyone you know needs an abortion, visit The Satanic Temple website at https://thesatanictemple.com/

As of this writing, Roe v. Wade is dangerously close to being overturned. The Satanic Temple website states they are "*Granting members the tools to receive medically safe abortions and protecting reproductive rights.*"

# Chapter One

# Flames Ain't Shit to a Demon

The constant fire raged, encompassing all of Armageddon. At the center of the flames stood Gertrude at her wheel. Gertrude was tired.

When it had come time for the fire to take everything, it was Gertrude who was called upon. Her purpose was to crank the wheel.

The wheel resembled a tall wagon wheel with a wooden handle. To make a full revolution, Gertrude would crank the splintered handle high over her head, extending her arms as far as she could, before pushing the handle down towards the ground, and lifting it back up again. The wheel was made torturously heavy by the iron chains it pulled from deep below the ground. Every cycle took all the strength and energy Gertrude had.

Cranking the wheel was all Gertrude had ever done, and all she was meant to do, but the fire and the hard labor had started to take its toll. The *Little House on the Prairie*-looking shit that she wore was tattered and dirty. Her handmade dress had holes and black marks from being singed by the fire. The matching bonnet that once covered her skull was now nothing but a rag.

Gertrude continued to crank the wheel, because it was her job to keep the fire burning. She looked at her hands and noted that much of the flesh had been rubbed off from the continuous turning of the handle, while the rest had started melting and dripping off in globs. The flesh she did have left on her hands was barely hanging on in a desperate attempt to stay attached.

Despite her new sensitivity to the heat, and the liquifying meat oozing off her body, she continued to try and turn the wheel. Her finger bones, now fully exposed and rife with arthritis, suddenly cracked and crumbled into dust, falling into the flames. She held up her fingerless hands and looked at them through eyes that were bulging out of her skinless face. She tried to keep the wheel moving by using her forearms, but it was a futile effort. The heavy chains weighed the wheel down, and it came to a screeching halt.

The all-encompassing flames of Armageddon started to retreat, once again pulling back towards the horizon, where they would cast their beautiful orange glow. As the roar of the fire started to lessen, a high-pitched screaming could be heard. The screaming had been going on ever since Gertrude started turning her wheel, but the roar of the fire had been too loud to notice.

As the flames retreated further, they revealed a small cottage with a large building behind it. Two people had been sitting on the front porch, screaming since the day the fires took hold. The cries of anguish finally came to an abrupt stop.

George and Rosemary sat in their rocking chairs, still holding hands, in the same spot they were before the fire had consumed everything. They looked at each other as their charred bodies started to slowly become recognizable again. When they could finally move and speak, Rosemary looked down at the broken glass at her feet.

"I wish I hadn't broken that glass. It was my favorite, and I'm awfully thirsty."

George looked at Rosemary and as they made eye contact, they both chuckled and he said, "Burning in eternal hellfire would make anyone a bit parched, I suppose. Let me go see if we have any sweet tea."

George stood up to go inside when they both noticed a dust storm in the distance. The ground started to shake a little, making George a little uneasy on his newly regenerated legs.

"Well," Rosemary said, "I guess there's no rest for the wicked. I wonder who that could be?"

## Chapter Two

# The First Church of Eve

Tonja sat at the front desk in the building that was referred to by the members as The Garden. It was a trailer that sat separate from all the other dorms on the ranch. She was scribbling on a yellow legal pad, daydreaming about getting the hell out of there.

To her right, through the kitchen, was Evelyn's bedroom. To her left was the master bedroom, where Cash and a select few of his favorite members spent most days shooting up and fucking.

The First Church of Eve was less of a church and more of a cult. "Every religion started out as a cult," Cash would say, "until they were around long enough that everyone forgot they were a cult and accepted them as a real religion. Just ask the Mormons."

Tonja didn't know what she expected when she agreed to help Cash "save the world," but she sure as shit was not expecting to play secretary for her brother's ego trip and Igor's junkie daughter.

Cash came walking out of his bedroom behind Chad and Lucy. He slapped them both on the ass as they walked out the front door in front of Tonja's desk. "Close your fucking bathrobe, Cash, I don't need to see my brother's dick. Again."

It was hard to tell when she could and couldn't make snide remarks at Cash. He inherited Earl's penchant for treating women like garbage, but at least Cash had never laid a hand on her. So, when she took a hard backhand across the face for her comments, it took her by surprise. She kept her head turned and looked to the floor as blood started to run from her lip. Her surprise turned into fuming anger, and she stood up to face Cash eye to eye.

"I don't have time for your bullshit, Tonja," Cash said as he turned away from her and waved her off. "It's almost time for nightly mass. Wake up Eve and get her down to the sanctuary. I want her to be there today."

Tonja watched as Cash went back into his room to start getting ready for his sermon. She wiped the blood from her lip and sniffled as she held back angry tears, then took a deep breath to collect herself. *I've had enough of this fucking bullshit,* she thought. Tonja had decided a long time ago she was done taking abuse from men.

She walked over to Eve's door and knocked.

***

Eve was 17 years old when Tonja and Cash showed up at her door. Eve lived with her mother, Amy. Things hadn't gone well for

Amy and Evelyn since the day Igor hung himself in the basement, where his little Evie watched him die.

Amy could never come up with a good reason why Igor killed himself and left his family behind. By all accounts, they had been a happy family. She never learned the truth about Igor, that he was the son of God and Satan. Or that his soul was an anomaly in this world, destined to suffer a worthless existence, forever and beyond, leaving everyone he came in contact with worse than before.

There were, of course, inklings that Igor was different. She had spent many nights constantly replaying the instance when a detective showed up at their house the night he killed himself. She always had a feeling that there was something significant about that event, but she just couldn't put her finger on it. Unbeknownst to Amy, the detective was the demon named Kristin. Kristin had been looking for Igor, and once she found him, she set his suicide in motion.

As would happen with just about anyone's life that Igor had been involved in, Amy's and Evelyn's lives quickly turned to shit. Amy started going out to bars, staying out late, drinking heavily, and leaving Evelyn home alone to fend for herself. They were evicted from the house Amy and Igor had bought together, and they moved into a rundown apartment complex on the south side of town.

It was during their time in apartment 316 that Roger started coming around. Roger could sniff out a broken woman from a mile away, and instinctively knew how to manipulate her. It didn't take long before he moved in with Amy and Evelyn permanently.

Alcohol had always been Amy's vice, and before meeting Roger, she had managed to stay away from any hard drugs. But Roger's main source of income was selling heroin. Roger was the one who offered to shoot her up for the first time. Soon after, Amy was more than comfortable with doing it herself.

With Amy's focus more on Roger and smack, she lost track of her daughter. Evelyn did whatever she wanted and had stopped going to school. She was 17 and, simply, no one gave a shit about her or what she was doing.

Roger liked to fuck with Evelyn. He liked to threaten her and push her around. He always hinted at violence and made sexual comments, but up until this point, he himself hadn't touched her or hurt her physically. Roger saved those privileges for his customers. Underage pussy was always an available upgrade on the menu.

One night, Evelyn was in her room with her door shut. She was lying on her bed, listening to music and sobbing quietly. Her entire life had been fucked up, and she just wanted to leave, but she had nowhere to go. She didn't have any friends or family to run to. She was stuck and didn't see a way out. She was considering following in her father's footsteps and killing herself, when Amy poked her head into her room.

"What's wrong, Evie? I thought I heard you crying."

"Don't fucking call me that!" Evelyn shouted through her sobs.

"Sorry honey, I know better." Amy walked into the room, looked around, and sat on the bed. She hadn't had a real conversation with her daughter in a very long time.

"Listen, I know things are fucked up. And I know that there are years' worth of feelings that you haven't had a fair chance to process and work through."

Evelyn turned and looked at her mother. She couldn't believe that Amy was actually talking to her, let alone trying to be a real mom. Evelyn sat up and leaned against the headboard of her bed. Her heart started beating a little faster as she felt a glimmer of hope. Maybe her mom still cared. Maybe there was a chance that they could get out of this fucked up situation they called a life. Maybe there would be another chance to start over.

"I feel like I've been so selfish," Amy continued. "I moved us into this shitty apartment. Roger is a fucking asshole. I'm just sorry, is all."

"It's okay, Mom. It is. It's okay." Evelyn wiped her nose with the sleeve of her shirt and started talking faster. "It's okay as long as we can get the hell out of here. There's still a chance to fix this Mom. We can escape this hell."

Evelyn looked her mother in the face for the first time in years, and she looked old. Older than she should. Evelyn saw the glassy look in Amy's eyes and could tell she was high. But she hoped maybe something she was saying was getting through to her.

"Escape. Right, you want to escape. Honey, that's why I'm here. And that's why I'm saying I'm sorry. I found the escape, baby. I *found* it and I left you behind."

Evelyn was still looking at her mom, still hopeful, but puzzled as to what she was talking about.

"I found the way out, Evie. And I want to share it with you. I want you to come with me, so we can escape together."

Before Evelyn could say anything about being called Evie, her mother showed her a zippered black bag that contained her needles.

Evelyn's heart sank into the darkest depths of human despair. For a few moments, her lungs forgot how to breathe. The shock ran through her and, in those few seconds, she was all but destroyed. She felt the last flicker of hope extinguish, never to return. It was replaced by an overwhelming anguish that she could feel in every part of her body. It was physically painful. It started in her chest and continued all the way to the tips of her fingers and her toes. She could feel the pain in the roots of her teeth and wanted to pull them all out.

Her mom didn't want to talk, or save her, or actually be a mother. She wanted to share her heroin with her daughter. Evelyn looked up through her tears and Roger was standing in the doorway, smiling. By the smug look on his face, she figured this was all his idea, but it didn't matter anymore. Nothing did.

"Whatever," Evelyn told her mother. She could barely get the words out, and they came out as no more than a whimper. It was impossible to utter another word. Her soul had crumbled and turned to dust. All she wanted now was for everything to just go away.

Evelyn stuck her arm out to her mother and turned her head. She felt Amy rolling her sleeve up, and the next thing she felt was a sense of euphoria, like she was being taken into the warm and welcoming arms of God herself, and then she fell asleep.

***

Three days before Evelyn's 18th birthday, Cash and Tonja knocked on the door of apartment 316.

"What a fucking shithole," Cash commented, while they waited for someone to answer the door.

"Who the fuck is it?!" a male voice finally yelled through the door. "If yer the pigs, you gotta tell me yer the pigs! That's my goddamn right to know!"

"We aren't the cops, man," Cash replied. "We are here for...business. It's cool. We're cool."

Roger unbolted the locks and cracked the door open just wide enough for him to see who was on the other side. "What kinda business are you talkin', boy? I don't know you."

Cash kicked the door open and sent Roger flying backwards onto the ground, where he landed on his side. Roger quickly stood up, ready to fight, but when he raised his head, he was staring down the barrel of Tonja's gun.

The commotion sort of woke Amy up. She was slouched over on the couch and, without opening her eyes, she mumbled, "It's the pumpkins, isn't it baby? The pumpkins are here for their revenge." No one acknowledged her.

"Who the fuck sent you? Was it Terry? I knew he'd try to fuckin' kill me one day!"

"It's not Terry, Roger, it's the fuckin' pumpkins!"

"Jesus Christ," Cash said with an exasperated tone. "We are not pumpkins, I don't know who the fuck Terry is, and we aren't going to kill you, unless you fuck us around. Where's Evelyn?"

"Oh," Roger said, both surprised and confused. "What the fuck do you want with that worthless bitch?"

Tonja put the gun to Roger's head and screamed, "None of your FUCKING business, asshole! Where is she?"

Roger had his hands up, but looked at Cash and said, "You better control your cunt, buddy."

Before Cash could respond, Tonja pistol-whipped Roger across the temple, and he fell back to the ground. Blood started running from the gash in his head, and Tonja put her foot on the wound and pressed down, making the blood pour out faster.

"Call me a cunt again," Tonja calmly demanded.

Roger was struggling and growling at the pain. His ears were ringing, and he was a little disoriented. When he didn't acknowledge Tonja, she squatted down next to him and pushed the wound on his head with the barrel of the gun.

"Hey, cocksucker. I said, call me a cunt again. I fucking dare ya."

"Alright, that's enough," Cash said. "Tonja, stand up and give this guy a chance to get himself together."

Roger sat up and leaned against the coffee table. He pointed towards a closed door down the hall. "That's her bedroom. Good luck."

Tonja gave the gun to Cash and knocked on Evelyn's door. When she didn't answer, Tonja let herself in. Evelyn was passed out on her bed with a needle still in her arm.

Tonja stood in the doorway feeling dejected. Evelyn looked like death, and the bed had fresh vomit running off the edge. *There she is,* Tonja thought, *our fucking savior.*

Tonja got Evelyn awake enough to walk her out into the living room. Evelyn shuffled in, leaning on Tonja, wearing pajama pants and an oversized sweatshirt.

"Oh fuck," Cash said when he saw Evelyn, "she's hooked on the junk, too?"

"Yep. I found her with a needle still in her arm."

Roger interjected. "She sure is. And she doesn't fucking pay for her shit, either."

"Whatever," Cash said, "let's just get her outta here." They started towards the door.

"Hold on, now. Just hold on one goddamn second," Roger had the balls to say as he stood up. "You can't just take a girl away from her family like this."

"Bye, Evie," Amy murmured from the couch.

Cash turned and looked at Roger. "Family? Really? Look at her. Look at what you've done to her and her mom. Fuck off, we're leaving and we're taking her with us."

"Well, okay, but she still owes me quite a bit for the smack. And if you leave without any of it, she's gonna get real sick, real fast. I think it's only fair that you pay me what she owes, plus buy some for the road."

Cash and Tonja made eye contact in the doorway and Cash once again turned back around. "Show me what you got and how much do I owe you?"

"Ah, see! I knew you were the reasonable one. This is why the men are in charge."

Tonja felt her muscles stiffen up and her jaw clench. She hated this motherfucker. He reminded her so much of her father.

"And since we are being reasonable, I think you should pay me for all the business I'm losing for you taking her. People come for the drugs, but they stay for that fine, young pussy."

Over on the couch, Amy was rambling on. "Can you hear them? Can you hear the screams and the cries of the pumpkins being slaughtered?"

Tonja's father, Earl, was a drunk who had beaten and raped her for most of her childhood. Tonja's mother, Sheila, stood by and let it happen. Much of the current situation reminded her of her past. Tonja sat Evelyn down on the chair next to the door.

Tonja pulled the gun out the back waistband of Cash's pants and shot Roger in the head. Pieces of skull and brain exploded all over the apartment. Cash, Tonja, and Amy were splattered with blood.

"What the fuck, Tonja?!" Cash screamed. "Holy shit!"

"How's that for fucking reasonable?"

On the couch, Amy opened her eyes and sat up. She was awake and alert, like she had never been high. Her eyes were opened wide and she looked at Cash and Tonja. It was as if she had suddenly become possessed.

"If you listen real close," Amy said as clear as day, "you can hear the screams of the pumpkins floating on the October breeze. It's a goddamn culling! A pumpkin holocaust!"

Tonja lifted the gun again and shot Amy right between her eyes. But instead of brains, pumpkin pulp and seeds splattered on the wall behind her. Cash and Tonja were now wearing blood and pumpkin guts.

"Fuck," Cash said, "just when you think things can't get any weirder."

Tonja gave the gun back to Cash, and he gathered up whatever drugs and money he could find. The police would surely be coming soon.

When Cash opened the door to leave, a flock of crows flew into the apartment. At least 15 or 20 birds temporarily overwhelmed the trio. Cash and Tonja crouched down to avoid getting hit in the head. The crows landed and started feeding on the brains and pumpkin seeds scattered about the living room.

Tonja and Cash gathered themselves, and then Tonja helped Evelyn get up. All the crows suddenly stopped cawing and feeding. They were completely still and utterly silent as they watched the three of them leave. Through her heroin haze, Evelyn could have sworn all the birds were looking at her.

***

"Did you really have to kill them both?" Cash asked Tonja, as he was driving down the road. Tonja was in the passenger seat and Evelyn was lying down, sleeping in the back.

"Neither of them deserved to live. Look at what they fucking did to her. The poor girl..."

"Don't you think this is how it would've ended up anyway? She is the daughter of Igor fucking Rotten..."

There was a pause in the conversation before Tonja spoke again, as they both pondered what it must be like to be Igor Rotten's daughter.

"So what's next? What do we do with her?" As Tonja spoke, she turned and looked back at Eve as she slept. She hadn't moved in a while, and she looked even paler than before.

"Oh, fuck!" Tonja exclaimed as she jumped between the seats and into the back. She struck Cash in the shoulder, making him swerve left of center. Thankfully, no one was coming the other way.

"What the hell, Tonja? What are you doing?"

Tonja was feeling around on Evelyn's neck for a pulse, but she already knew. Her body was colder than it should be.

"She's fucking dead, Cash."

***

"Are you fucking kidding me? After all this, she's fucking dead?"

Cash had pulled the car over on the side of the road. Tonja was in the backseat holding Evelyn's head in her lap, crying. Tonja didn't know Evelyn personally, but she empathized with her and the shit she had gone through. Tonja had secretly hoped that maybe she could save Evelyn from herself, and teach her to cope with the horrific trauma she had experienced.

"I really thought she would be able to help us, somehow. She's the fuckin' granddaughter of God and Lucifer, for fuck's sake." Cash was pacing around outside the passenger side of the car. The back door was open and he looked in disbelief at Tonja holding Evelyn's body. He put his hands on top of his head and looked up to the sky, thinking about what to do next.

"We have to get rid of the body, Tonja. If they find us with her body, they will know what we...well, what you did at the apartment."

"Hey, what the fuck, Cash? Are you already thinking about how to blame all this shit on me? All that time in the ether really fucked you up, didn't it?"

Evelyn opened her eyes and took a deep, gasping breath, and then began to cough. Tonja and Cash just stared with their mouths open as she sat up having a coughing fit. Through her coughs, she looked them both with the dumbfounded looks on their faces and asked, "How about a drink of water?"

Tonja reached up front, grabbed the bottle of water she was drinking earlier, and gave it to Evelyn. She chugged it down and eventually stopped coughing. Tonja and Cash were still staring in bewilderment.

"What?"

"You were definitely dead," Tonja said. "She was definitely dead, right Cash?"

"Very fucking dead," Cash verified.

Evelyn simply said, "Uh...surprise?"

Cash's eyes lit up and a smirk appeared on his face. "You know, you might be more like your father than you think."

***

It was time for the nightly mass at The First Church of Eve. Tonja was sitting in her spot on the stage, to the left of where Cash stood at his podium. She was still fuming about how Cash had hit her across the face. She *swore* she would never let another man abuse her.

Behind Cash, there sat a raised platform with an old recliner. It was supposed to be a throne, but the budget warranted finding a used recliner on the side of the road. In the chair sat Eve, the supposed savior of them all.

Eve was draped in an oversized, white, frilly nightgown Chad had found at the Goodwill in town. She wore a crown made of ivy and twine. She was trying to keep her eyes open during Cash's sermon.

In what was supposed to be a plan to defeat the evil that was to be unleashed on the world, Tonja and Cash had effectively started a cult that was centered around Eve as their savior. To date, forty-six men and women believed Cash when he told the story that Eve had risen from the dead. They came to the ranch to be saved, but stayed for the heroin. Everyone there but Tonja was hooked on the stuff, and selling it was the only way The First Church of Eve made any money.

Tonja peered out at the forty-six-person congregation. They were either sitting on steel folding chairs or old patio furniture, and she was certain most of them had no idea what the hell was going on anymore. She felt a little bad for them. Like her, they listened to Cash's bullshit and ended up here. She was deep in her own thoughts when something in Cash's sermon caught her attention.

"...and that's why I believe the next step in being saved, the next step in turning our quaint little ranch into The Garden of Eden, is to give our Eve...an Adam! And through God's communication to Eve, which she has since communicated to me, I know what I must do."

Cash continued excitedly. "There's going to be a ceremony! There's going to be a wedding! Three days from now, Eve and I will be married. And after I have taken her hand, and consummated our marriage, I will no longer be Cash. From that moment forward, I will be known as Adam!"

Cash stood with his hands in the air, looking up at the dilapidated ceiling of the sanctuary, with a wide smile on his face. A few people from the congregation gave half-hearted claps to express their excitement.

Tonja couldn't believe what the fuck she was hearing. Until recently, Cash had at least pretended she was still a part of...whatever this was. Oh, how things had changed. He never mentioned a word of this to her.

Cash walked up to the throne, took Eve by the hands, and helped her stand up. She didn't put up a struggle as Cash kissed her on the lips, and then raised both of their hands above their heads, like they had won something or were about to take a bow. A few more of the faithful had come to life, and there was some more clapping, along with some sporadic hoots and hollers.

Tonja had, up until this point, shown more restraint than she was known for. And, you know, brother or not, she *swore* she would never let another man abuse her.

Tonja got up, unnoticed, and went into the storage room in the back of the sanctuary. She and Cash were the only two with keys to the room, and for good reason. Behind the door was where they kept a small arsenal, just in case someone came along and tried to steal their drugs or threaten their "way of life." Tonja opened the door, slung an assault rifle over her shoulder, and looked around for her favorite handgun. She found it and put it in her waistband. She filled a duffle bag with some ammunition and shut the door again.

Cash had led Eve down to the podium. He still had a wide, bright smile on his face. He was almost orgasmic with his mouth wide open, showing his not-so-white teeth. No matter what he really thought, he made these people believe Eve was their savior and he was God's prophet. But in this place, he was God.

About half of the congregation were now standing and applauding. Some were crying. They were all so happy. And why wouldn't they be? There was going to be a wedding, after all.

Tonja walked up behind Cash and Eve. No one was paying attention to her. She had been in the background of this whole thing for so long, she had nearly become invisible. If anyone had been paying attention to her, they might have tried to warn Cash that a woman with a gun was looming behind him. She stood there for a few seconds and watched him soak in the adoration of the brainwashed junkies.

Tonja grabbed Cash by the shoulder and spun him around to face her. His eyes were still wide open with the big, dumb smile across his face. His euphoria was interrupted when Tonja stuck her favorite handgun, the one she used to kill Roger and Amy, into Cash's mouth. She saw a split second of realization in his eyes before she pulled the trigger.

The bullet blew out the back of his head, which caused some blood, skull, and brain to splatter all over the first few rows of the forty-six. There was a moment of surprised silence after the gunshot, followed by the thud of Cash's body hitting the ground. It was a bit of an awkward silence until Lucy let out a scream, and the congregation started frantically running around, unsure of what to do.

Eve, who was sobered up by the adrenaline, looked at Tonja in shock, expecting to be next in line to die. Instead, Tonja grabbed her by the arm and just said, "Let's go."

Tonja and Eve made their way towards the door when Tonja saw Chad, Lucy, and a few of Cash's other favorites banding together and pointing at her. They started to make their way towards Tonja and Eve in a jog, so Tonja whipped her assault rifle around and unloaded indiscriminately into the scurrying congregation. Blood splattered and bullets ripped through a countless number of limbs and organs. Chad and Lucy were killed, along with some other members of the First Church of Eve. The rest scattered in the opposite direction, and Tonja once again grabbed Eve by the wrist and led her out the door.

Tonja took Eve and headed towards the Garden. She was going to load up whatever drugs and money were in the safe and grab the keys to Cash's car. While most of the congregation had fled, there were three of them that saw an opportunity inside

The Garden. They were rifling through drawers and closets, presumably looking for drugs. Tonja didn't hesitate and mowed down two wide-eyed men and a woman who tried to scream but never had the chance. Bullets blew through the cheap trailer walls and sprayed them with blood as the bodies collapsed to the floor.

Eve looked on in fright, unable to speak. She was sober and scared. She either wanted to run or get high, but she thought if she tried to run, Tonja would kill her like she did everyone else.

Another woman slowly walked out of Eve's bedroom with her hands in the air. She was afraid and crying, and blubberingly began to beg for her life. Before Tonja could be bothered to hear what she had to say, she ripped her apart with bullets, spraying her insides back into Eve's bedroom.

"Jesus Christ!" Eve finally said through tears. "Why are you killing all these people? Cash may have deserved it, but these people were brainwashed and drugged up. They could be...they could have been good people!"

Tonja looked at Eve with a blank face and shrugged her shoulders as she reloaded the rifle. "I guess it's up to God to sort them all out, isn't it?"

Eve cried while Tonja went to the safe and filled the bag with heroin and a few stacks of money. "We've got money and a car. And we've got some smack to keep you from getting sick. Are you coming with me or not?"

Eve considered her options once again. She took another look at Tonja, with her weapons in hand. She had a numb, yet impatient, look on her face. You wouldn't have thought by looking at her that she just murdered a group of people.

Eve didn't have any other ideas on what she should do, so she agreed to go along with Tonja. They walked outside and got in Cash's car. They drove off on the dirt road leading away from the ranch, with no plans on where to go next.

# Chapter Three

# The First Trumpet of Revelation

Mary was passed out and slumped over on the couch. She was snoring. Her housecoat was open and her legs were spread, with her unkempt pubic hair showing. It didn't matter, there was no one else around. Jim was gone, but she was still tucked away in her interdimensional prison.

The myriad of television monitors in front of her were all off the air, showing the static snow, and blaring white noise. She had grown weary of watching anything to do with what was happening on Earth. She didn't turn her water into wine anymore; she was turning it into 190 proof grain alcohol just to knock herself out.

What woke her from her drunken slumber was a heavy crack of thunder, followed by what sounded like a trumpet.

"Was that...?" she groggily asked herself out loud. "No, it couldn't be..."

But it could be. And it was. There was no other sound that could have emanated from outside the prison that she would have heard.

# Chapter Four

# Theatre of the Mind

Over the edges of no place to go, in the space between reality and dream, exists a movie theatre. Ok, so it doesn't ACTUALLY exist. Because *there* is really *nowhere* at all, but Igor Rotten's consciousness ended up there. Which is nowhere. You get it.

Anyway, his consciousness, without a body or a soul, had to create a familiar environment to exist. And so, Igor Rotten's Theatre of the Mind was constructed. Along with the theatre came its very own cinephile, Todd.

Todd was a skinny man who wore thin glasses and a watch that doubled as a calculator. He liked to tuck his faded blue polo into his mildly wrinkled khakis. He was going bald on top of his head but had a sweet, sweet ponytail flowing down his back.

In the projection room, Todd had a collection of films in canisters that took up an entire wall of shelves. He had a ladder on wheels that he could use to reach the topmost canisters. His ponytail would cinematically blow in the gentle breeze as the ladder rolled him from one end of the shelves to the other.

None of the film canisters were labeled, because Todd had memorized the entire catalog. He knew which films were stored in which spot without having to think twice.

The theatre itself had one seat, and it was for Igor. Igor was strapped in what looked like a strait jacket, unable to move, and was forced to watch whatever film Todd decided to show him. To make sure Igor didn't close his eyes, Todd used clamps to hold each of Igor's eyelids open.

"What the fuck is going on here, Todd?" Igor had only just arrived and was becoming aware of his surroundings. "And how do I know your name is Todd?"

Todd turned away from Igor to grab the eye drops, and the end of his ponytail scratched Igor's eye.

"Ahh! Goddamnit, Todd!"

"Sorry there, Igor. This golden mane has a mind of its own sometimes. Let me put a couple drops in your eyes to soothe the pain."

"What the fuck is going on here, Todd?" Igor asked again. "Are you...are you like, Clockwork Orange-ing me?"

"In a few minutes, we'll begin your treatment. You're a very lucky boy to have been chosen," Todd recited.

"Very funny. Are you going to give me a shot that makes me sick at the sight of rape and ultra-violence?"

“Something like that, Igor. Except there’s no shot. I am just going to show you some movies.”

Igor involuntarily responded, “Like going to the pictures?”

“Something like that.”

“Well, that’s good. I like to viddy the old films now and again. Wait, Todd, what the fuck did I just say? Why did I say that?”

Todd started the film. It was a recording of Igor’s last moments alive. He was in Bethany’s house, trying to kill her for hating soup. Plus, he needed her tongue for the daughter he was building from spare body parts. Igor planned to reanimate the body he was constructing with the soul of his daughter, Evie.

After watching the horrific events he had personally perpetrated on poor Bethany, he started to scream.

“Don’t make me watch this, Todd. I’m going to be sick. Let me be sick, Todd! I want to get up. Get me something to be sick in! Oh, God...”

Igor continued to beg as he felt worse, like he was going to die. “Stop the films, Todd. Please stop it! I can’t stand it anymore. Stop it, please! Please...”

“I can’t stop this, Igor. I can’t. I see you and I wish I could, but I can’t. I can’t because you made this. In fact, you made me. You created this entire place. This is how you think you deserve to spend eternity.”

Igor watched the screen as Bethany bashed his skull in with a can of soup, and the film reel spun to the end. He felt a sense of relief until Todd went to the projector to start the next film.

On screen, Igor was standing on a chair in the basement, preparing to hang himself, while his daughter Evie watched him from the bottom of the stairs.

# Chapter Five

# Oblivions

Oblivion is a spirit realm that exists somewhere between Hell and Armageddon. It has an unforgiving desert landscape, and is occupied by wayward angels, demons, and other outlaw spirits that defy the standard rules of human life and death. It's a purgatory, of sorts.

In Oblivion, the scorching sun never sets and there's never a cloud in the sky. The wind constantly churns to cause violent sandstorms. Particles of sand swirl through the air, roughing up the residents' skin and blinding their eyes. Even if an occupant of Oblivion finds the occasional shelter from the hot sun and sand, the commotion outside is so loud, there's little chance of sleep. There truly is no rest for the wicked.

Vegetation is rarely seen, and water is rarely found. The only plentiful source of hydration is whiskey. Whiskey flows from the never-ending taps at The Raven's Den. The Den is located in the center of Oblivion and is both a whiskey bar and an inn. If you're one of the lucky few inhabitants of Oblivion, you are extended credit at The Den, and can occasionally get a room for the night. If you're drunk enough, you might even get a few hours of sleep.

Time doesn't mean much in Oblivion. The landscape and the company of other outlaw souls age you mentally and physically, faster than a calendar ever could. So, it's hard to say just how long James had called Oblivion home. By his tan, leathery skin, and crow's feet around his eyes, you'd have guessed him to be a hard-drinking middle-aged man. Maybe he was.

Jamie, as the residents of Oblivion called him, was lying on the ground outside of The Raven's Den. He had an empty bottle of whiskey that he had managed to steal loosely clenched in his fist, and vomit dried from the corner of his mouth and down his cheek. Three crows were picking through the vomit near his head, searching for some sort of sustenance. His pants were quickly drying in the sun, but it was evident to the demons, Tristan and Elias, who were standing over him, that Jamie had pissed himself.

"It's a fuckin' shame," Tristan said.

"The grandson of the almighty God and Lucifer," Elias said with grandiosity and sarcasm, "in all his fucking glory!"

Tristan laughed, "Kristin must be *sooooo* proud!"

"Takes after his daddy, I guess," Elias said with a chuckle. Both of them walked away, leaving Jamie to be pelted by the blowing sand and broiled by the ferocity of the sun.

Jamie's eyes popped open, staring through the dust-riddled gusts of wind and into the eternally bright sun. The crows that had been picking through his puke immediately took to the skies and flew towards the unsuspecting demon duo of Tristan and Elias. The crows circled around their heads, swooping down and back around, avoiding the waving hands and ignoring the screams to stop.

"What the shit?!" Tristan yelled as he simultaneously swatted at the air and crouched down.

Elias screamed and cowered, waving his arms above his head. "Ah! I fuckin' hate birds!"

The crows made their pass, and once again circled around and swooped downward towards their faces. This time, one of the crows caught Elias and left two deep scratches across his already heavily scarred face. Another crow caught Tristan by the hair and ripped a chunk of it out of his scalp. Blood trickled down his forehead.

Amidst the confusion, Jamie had gotten himself off the ground and walked up behind Tristan. Tristan was focused on the sky, waiting for another bird attack, when Jamie grabbed him by the shoulder and turned him around. Jamie took the empty whiskey bottle and belted Tristan across the face, breaking his jaw and knocking him to the ground.

Elias was several feet away, still flailing his arms. When he turned, he saw Jamie standing over Tristan, bludgeoning him a second, and then a third time, in the skull. Blood splattered on Jamie's face and Tristan's head started to leak into the sand.

Elias charged toward Jamie and hit him at full speed with his shoulder. Jamie wasn't a big guy, but Elias was, and Jamie flew backwards onto the hard ground. The crows once again intervened and distracted Elias long enough for Jamie to recover and get back to his feet. He smashed the bottle on a nearby rock, which caused it to break. Elias rushed toward Jamie once again, but this time when he tackled him, he fell on top of Jamie.

Elias's face was inches away from Jamie's, his mouth hanging open, and his eyes wide with surprise. Jamie's broken bottle had caught him in the side of the stomach, and Elias's own weight and momentum forced the jagged glass deep inside him.

Blood started to run from Elias's mouth onto Jamie's lips. Jamie ran his tongue over his own lips several times and licked up the blood droplets. He smirked as he watched the life start to slowly fade from the demon's eyes.

It took nearly all his strength to push Elias's fat ass off of him. Jamie stood up and put his foot on the bottle's neck, slowly pushing it even farther into Elias's guts. Blood poured faster from Elias's mouth as he tried to scream, but the gurgling of blood in his throat was all that could be heard.

Satisfied that Elias wasn't going anywhere, Jamie put his hands on his hips and took a deep breath of the hot Oblivion air. It wasn't at all refreshing, and it made him double over and cough. He looked over at Tristan and watched as two of the crows pecked at his eyes. The third crow was eating his brain through a crack in his skull.

Jamie got on his knees near Elias and wanted to watch him slowly die. But the crows, now with four of them in their murder, flew over and landed near Elias. They watched Jamie, expectantly, and finally he sighed and said, "Ok, fine." The crows swarmed onto Elias and began to eat his soft parts while he was still clinging to the little bit of life he had left.

Jamie sat back against the same rock that he used to break the bottle and watched as the crows took Elias apart, eyes first. One of the crows was pulling at his tongue and got a piece loose. The bird flew over to Jamie and landed on his shoulder, the piece of tongue still hanging from its beak. Jamie opened his mouth and the crow fed it to him.

"Thanks, bud," Jamie said, chewing.

Minutes later, Elias died, and the group of crows now numbered five. Jamie stood up and said, "Well, fellas, I'm thirsty. Let's see what's going on inside the Raven's Den, shall we?"

***

James found himself in Oblivion for simply being the typical asshole teenager, who just happened to be the grandson of both God and Satan. When Igor was finally gone and permanently out of the way, Kristin was more than happy to let Jim groom James into becoming the single most evil being the world had ever known. And even though Jim had been the most feared entity in all the worlds; Lucifer, The Fallen Angel, King of the Underworld,

The Serpent, The Tempter of Man, etc., even The Dark Lord himself found it difficult to raise a fucking teenager.

"You're going to join the goddamn military, and that's final!" Jim yelled at James. "That's always been the plan, and that's still the motherfucking plan!"

"Yeah, I know the plan!" James hollered back. "Rise through the ranks, become influential, start wars, and end this fucking place. I get it. But that's *your* vision for my life, Grandpa. What about *my* vision?"

"Indulge me, boy," Jim said, obviously feigning interest. "What is your vision for your life? What could be better than fulfilling your birthright and bringing on the end of the *fucking* world!"

James looked at Satan himself with a straight face and said, "If you must know...I want to be a filmmaker."

The Devil looked at his grandson like he just caught him saying his goodnight prayers. James continued, despite the look of absolute disgust. "I have some good ideas, Grandpa, and I can already see the scenes in my head. I have this one idea for a movie ---"

"Enough," Jim interrupted, with an exasperated whisper. He stood with his eyes closed and took a deep breath, trying to keep his composure. "Not only are you going into the military, like I fucking said, but I'm calling the local recruiter. In less than a week, you're going to be at a private military school. They will beat this idiotic idea out of your head, and you're staying there until you're old enough to go off to boot camp!"

James was devastated. He tried to argue his point as Jim walked away and, for a moment, Jim lost his temper and turned back around. Jim's face was no longer masked in his human form. His human flesh melted away, and the face of a fallen angel that had been burning since the dawn of time showed through. His forked tongue spewed from his mouth as he screamed, "I SAID ENOUGH!" A few droplets of acidic saliva expelled from Jim's mouth and landed on James's skin, burning him.

While Jim's face was terrifying, it was what James saw in his grandfather's eyes that really scared him. With Jim's mask being ripped away, James saw the true capacity of evil that lurked inside his grandfather. Sure, they talked all the time about how great it would be to bring about The Ultimate Suffering, but it was another thing to see it. Satan's eyes swirled with the hunger for the eternal pain and agony for all living things. As James continued to look into his eyes, he could see Jim's plans for him playing out. The indiscriminate suffering James was meant to usher forth made the bile in his stomach rise up in his throat. He took a few steps back, horrified at what he had just seen. Talking about horrific acts in theory, and seeing them in practice, are two different things and James wasn't prepared to see what was meant to happen.

Jim hadn't been in his true form for what seemed like an eternity, but an argumentative teenager finally forced it out of him (which is something many parents can identify with). Jim turned and walked away, reigning in his anger and returning to his full human form. It took James a moment to regroup before he turned slowly and went to his room, shutting the door behind him.

***

Jim wasn't bluffing when he said he was sending James to military school. Nine days after the argument, the local recruiter, Sergeant Williams, was scheduled to pick James up from his house.

During those nine days, all James could think about was what he had seen in the eyes of Lucifer. He saw himself riding a pale horse, trotting on a path of flames that reached up to his knees; the sun blotted out by the smoke from the hellfire that burned. He sat on his horse with his back straight and his head held high, holding the reins. His eyes were blackened as he faced straight ahead, unphased by all the anguish around him.

The path of flames was carved through incalculable piles of dead bodies. Bodies of men, women, and children alike wore scorched flesh from which their liquified internal organs leaked. Demons and hellhounds fed on the flesh that easily fell off the bones, like perfectly cooked baby back ribs.

The path lined with fire led to his throne which was constructed from the bones of angels. An uncountable number of crows rested atop the throne, and more flew in circles above, against the backdrop of a black and red sky. James took his seat, and to his left was his grandfather, sitting on his own throne, basking in the glory of a job well done. To his right was a garden that composed of the heads of their enemies and detractors. Prominently displayed on a stake was the head of a woman whom he had never met, but he knew it was his half-sister, Eve. Next to her was the head of Mary, the grandmother of both Eve and James, who also just happened to be God.

This glimpse into the future scared the shit out of James, and he knew he didn't want to be the one to bring about the end of the world, but he remained paralyzed with fear until there was a knock on his bedroom door.

"James, you better have your shit packed," Jim said through the door. "Sergeant Williams is here to take you to the school."

When James didn't answer, Jim opened the door and walked in with Sergeant Williams behind him. James was still lying on the bed, staring up at the ceiling. He had not, in fact, had his shit packed.

Sergeant Williams was a scumbag recruiter who didn't feel at all bad for talking teenagers into joining the military, and possibly dying in pointless wars. As soon as his recruits left for bootcamp, he promptly forgot about them. They were just another number towards the quota he was expected to meet.

So, he really didn't care about the argument Jim was having with James. In fact, he was annoyed by it. It was his job to get James from there to the school, and after that, he'd most likely never think about him again. He tuned out the argument completely, and instead he started to daydream about the woman with the big ass and tight yoga pants he saw at the gas station while he was fueling up his Hummer. *I should have just talked to her instead of coming here,* he thought. *I could have that ass in my face right now.*

That was the last thought Sergeant Williams ever had.

During the argument, James had grabbed an ancient sword that hung on his wall. It had been used during The Crusades and was given to him by his grandfather for his 8th birthday. "I'm not going!" James screamed as he swung the sword at Sergeant Williams. One swing sliced his head right off.

"You little BASTARD!" Jim roared. This time, his full human form didn't just melt away, his flesh instantly turned to ashes amongst the flames of Lucifer's anger. There, in James's bedroom, stood Satan in his true form. His black wings spread from wall to wall as he took his clawed fist and grabbed James by the throat. Satan watched blissfully as James, eyes wide with surprise and fear, struggled for his life. As James choked, the claws of Lucifer dug in deeper. James's body began to take on a deep orange glow, quickly turning his flesh to a charred black. The insides of James liquified in the heat and began to flow from his body and onto the floor like lava pouring out of a volcano. Soon, James was no more than a heap of thick, flaming liquid.

"Ah, fuck," Jim said once he had gained his composure and returned to human form. He looked down at what used to be his grandson, threw his hands in the air, and then put his hands on his hips. "This," Jim said aloud. "This is...unfortunate."

"It sure FUCKING is."

Jim was startled by the woman's voice. He turned around and looked at the demon Kristin who was, more importantly, James' mother.

Jim started to apologize for killing her son, but Kristin had already sprinted forward and, before he knew it, she had her arms around him, pulling him to the ground. When he hit the floor, he was still in James' bedroom. But a moment later, he was in what appeared to be basement.

# Chapter Six

# The Second Trumpet of Revelation

Saint Peter was manning his post at the gates of Heaven. He was busy with the rush of souls that had been arriving. The line seemed to be infinitely long. He was dealing with one particularly loud fuckhead named Brad who was wearing a Guns, God, and Country shirt when he bit the dust. Pete was going over his litany of sins to judge if he was worthy of entering the gates.

"Why would you tell the referee at a high school football game that he should be 'Hung by the neck until dead.'"

Brad got red in the face, not from embarrassment, but from anger. "That sonofabitch cost my boy his only chance at a touchdown! It was pass interference, and a blind man could have seen it!"

"Your son's team was 0-8, and they were losing 42-0," Pete said. "Your son, along with the rest of the team, sucked. That wasn't the ref's fault."

"I don't care if you're a saint, you take that back right now."

Pete snapped his fingers and the *Star Spangled Banner* began to play. Brad quickly took off his camouflage ball cap and covered his heart. He turned in a circle, desperately looking for the United States flag.

"You're a fuckin tool, Brad, but honestly the bar for entry has been lowered so much, I think you'll fit right in. There's a cooler full of Coors Light waiting for you on the other side of the gates. Enjoy."

Pete looked up at the next contestant on this never-ending shit show, when he saw a crazy-looking woman with nappy hair, an open robe, and nothing underneath running towards him. He was about to tell her to take her crazy ass to the back of the line and wait her turn when he recognized her.

"Mary?"

"Pete," she said, trying to catch her breath, "Pete, you need to let me back in. "

"Mary, how did you get out of prison?"

"Come on, Pete. I'm God for fuck's sake. I could have left whenever I wanted."

"Well, I'm under strict instructions to not let you through these gates."

Mary was about to unleash holy hell on Pete, when the sound of the second trumpet blared throughout Heaven. The souls in line covered their ears and screamed in agony. Mary and Pete just looked at each other.

"Oh fuck!" Pete exclaimed.

"Oh fuck, indeed."

# Chapter Seven

# The Thrilling of Claire

Tonja had been driving for hours. Eve sat in the passenger seat with her head against the window, slipping in and out of sleep. She had used a little bit of heroin to fight the sickness of withdrawal she felt coming on. She had already been trying to wean herself off for the last few months, but it just wasn't working. She needed help, but she didn't even have any identification. She was a ghost in this world, and if she died, who would notice?

Tonja was tired and had no idea where she was going. She understood that the desert got colder at night, but in the last few miles, the temperature had dropped dramatically. She had turned on the heat in the car, but she could still see her breath. As if the heat not working wasn't bad enough, she looked down at her gas gauge and saw she was almost out of fuel. Just as she accepted that they were going to run out of gas in the middle of fucking nowhere, she saw the glow of a gas station sign up ahead.

Tonja's car coasted into the lot and stopped at the pump. If the station had been another quarter mile down the road, they would have been pushing the car. Tonja pumped their fuel and then roused Evelyn. They both went inside to grab some snacks and pay for the gas.

The clerk at the counter was an older woman. She was sitting in a chair at the register, with her feet on the counter, reading a trash romance novel. The bell from the door startled her when Tonja and Eve walked through it. Tonja noticed it was really fucking cold in there too.

"Why the fuck is it so goddamn cold?" Tonja asked the cashier.

"Well, a sudden drop in temperature is sometimes an omen," said the old woman. "It usually means something, how should I say it, *significantly* bad is going to happen. I noticed the change a just few moments ago. Then you two showed up."

"Bitch, I could be the worst thing that ever happened to you," Tonja snapped back.

The old woman behind the counter wasn't having any of Tonja's shit. "Oh, fuck you, you little twat. I'm not worried about you. I'm worried about her."

The woman pointed toward Eve, who was standing behind Tonja, wrapped in her favorite oversized hooded sweatshirt, only half paying attention to what was happening. Eve just stared at the woman, stuttering until Tonja interrupted.

"Twat? Who are you calling a twat, you old bitch. You better just shut your fucking mouth until we pay for our shit and get the fuck out of here. Keep it up and this will become a really bad night for you."

The old woman hadn't stopped looking at Eve. She brushed off Tonja with a wave of her hand, much like Cash did before, and barely acknowledged the threats to her life.

Tonja stepped back and finally noticed the weird connection Eve and this woman had. She watched as they stared at each other, and had no idea what the hell was happening, but she didn't like it. Tonja started again, annoyed by this whole thing, before she was interrupted.

"What in THEE fuck is going on h---"

"Have either of you ever participated in a seance before? You know, for fun," the old woman asked. She said 'either of you,' but she was still looking at Eve.

"Maybe we should just go, Eve," Tonja said in a much more reasonable tone now. She was getting concerned. She had seen plenty of fucked up shit happen and wasn't in the mood to witness anymore tonight.

"No. I think we should have a seance." Eve broke the trance that she and the woman were in to look at Tonja. "You know, for fun."

The woman smiled and led them through a door to the back room.

***

The woman, who had now identified herself as Claire, sat between Tonja and Eve. They were sitting around a circular table made of a heavy marble with swirling blue, green, and black tones. There were dozens of candles lit throughout the room. Claire had changed into a draping robe and looked more like a stereotypical fortune teller you'd see on television.

"Before we start," Claire announced, "it'll be 500 bucks."

Claire claimed to be a spiritual medium. She really did have some sort of connection between the spirit realms and the physical world, and on some level, she knew that. When she was young, she had to see a child psychologist because she told her parents she could talk to dead people. Booze, medication, and adulthood had numbed her senses enough to where she hadn't felt anything supernatural in at least thirty years. She kept up the ruse to scam housewives out of their money, but she felt *something* when Eve walked through the door of her little service station on the side of the road.

"Are you fucking kidding me?" Tonja said in an exasperated tone. "500 bucks? What a fucking rip-off! Eve, are you really going to fall for this shit?"

"Just pay her. Please?"

"Fuck, fine," Tonja groaned. She took a stack of cash out of her bag and gave it to Claire. Tonja had seen the weird connection Claire and Eve had, and deep down, she wanted to see what it was all about.

Claire noticed the rest of the cash in the bag and made a mental note to try and scam them out of the rest before they left.

"Ok, first let's all hold hands," Claire said.

Tonja rolled her eyes. "Jesus Christ, did you take this bit straight from a movie?"

"Tonja, come on! Just do it. Please?," Eve begged. Tonja had never seen Eve act this way. She never saw her act any way but high, once she thought about it. All this time together, and they really didn't know each other at all.

"Hands, please!" Claire demanded, interrupting Tonja's train of thought.

The three of them held hands in a circle around the table. Claire closed her eyes and started her dramatic diatribe to the dead.

"Hear me now, those in the worlds beyond. Tonja and Eve are here, and if there's anyone with a message for them, make me your vessel. Speak to Tonja. Speak to Eve. I am at your disposal."

This was the part where she would pretend a spirit had entered her, and ask leading questions of her customers to figure out who they really wanted to speak to. She didn't have to pretend this time.

The temperature in the room dropped so fast that Tonja's sweaty palms felt like they were going to freeze together with Claire's and Eve's. Claire's head flipped back so hard, Eve thought her head could have broken off her neck. Her eyes glossed over as she looked straight up at the ceiling. A dry, continuous moan emanated from her throat.

Tonja and Eve had let go of each other's hands in an attempt to back away, but Claire had an unnaturally strong grip on both of them. They looked at her with terrified wonder as her head went from looking straight up, to forcefully snapping down and facing the table. Then, she turned her head towards Tonja. Tonja saw Claire's eyes were nothing but a cloudy white, but she still appeared to be peering directly into Tonja's most intimate thoughts. It was a scrutiny that she found strangely familiar, uncomfortable, and filled her with fear. She knew before Claire spoke that she wasn't Claire anymore. She knew who was looking at her before she heard his voice coming from Claire's throat.

"Ah, there's my little girl," Earl said. Claire still looked like Claire, but she also looked exactly like her dead father.

"I've missed you, but most of all, I've missed your tight little cunt."

Claire/Earl reared their head back and laughed. Tonja tried again to pull away but the grip on her was unbreakable. She was a helpless little girl again as she pulled as hard as she could, trying to get away, crying and panicking.

Through Earl's laugh, she heard another voice. It was Sheila, her mother. "You little whore! You shot me in the head, and you're still trying to steal your daddy away from me! You fucking slut!"

"Oh yeah, she's a slut alright!" Earl screamed. "She lies in her room at night touching herself, wishing Daddy would come home. Don't you, Tonja? Don't you wish Daddy would come home?"

Claire's head cocked sideways as her wet tongue pushed through and licked her lips, slowly and deliberately, all the way around.

"All this time, Tonja, and I've never forgotten how you taste."

The room shook as Eve watched Tonja scream and cry. She never stopped trying to pull her hand away, and Claire's nails had dug into Tonja's forearms so deep, blood was pouring onto the table.

Eve was horrified at what she was watching and let out a scream. Her voice didn't seem to be hers. It was louder and deeper than any human's voice should go. She screamed, "STOP!" Her voice reverberated throughout the building and suddenly the room stopped shaking. Claire immediately raised her head and was once again staring at the ceiling, completely calm, but her grip on their wrists was still intact. Eve was breathing heavily, sucking in the ice cold air, thinking about how the hell she just made that sound. Tonja was whimpering, still trying to pry Claire's fingers from inside her forearm.

Claire turned her head towards Eve.

"I don't want to watch it again!" Claire said in a man's voice. "Don't make me watch it again."

Claire finally let go of both women. They were free but couldn't help but be mesmerized by what was happening. Claire stood up, picked up her chair, and set it down on its legs in the middle of the table.

"Please, no," the male voice pleaded through Claire. "Please don't make me watch it again."

Claire climbed on top of the chair and took off her scarf. She tied one end to the wooden beam running underneath the ceiling. She tied a noose on the other end and put it around her neck. She turned and looked at Eve with her clouded eyes.

"Oh, Evie. Don't watch. Please, just turn around."

Eve hadn't heard that voice since she was a little girl. The last time she heard it was when her father, Igor Rotten, hung himself in front of her down in their basement.

Eve put her hands over her mouth and backed up against the wall as she watched it all happen again. Claire kicked the chair out from under herself, and the noose tightened around her neck. She was kicking and struggling as she choked to death, but her eyes never blinked as she gazed at Eve.

Tonja had slowly moved over next to Eve, and they held each other as they both watched Claire gasp for air. Claire grabbed at her neck and kicked her feet for what felt like an eternity. Then her body went limp.

"What the fuck just happened here?" Tonja softly asked through her tears. Eve couldn't muster a response, so she turned and buried her face in Tonja's shoulder. Tonja halfheartedly hugged her, as she began to try and process everything that had just happened. However, neither of them would get the chance. Claire's body, still hanging from the rafters, started to convulse.

Both Tonja and Eve looked up at Claire's corpse as it thrashed around erratically. A high-pitched, continual tone rang throughout the room as Claire's proverbial third eye became literal, and started to form in the middle of her forehead. It pushed through her skull like a baby bird pushing its way out of an egg. Claire was dead, but the eye was alive and frantically looking around the room.

Claire's skin turned a dark gray, like the flesh was rotting at an accelerated rate, yet it began to crack like it had hardened into stone. A bright white light started showing through the cracks in her skin. The light was followed by the flow of blood and chunks of bone and organs. Claire's entire body was now breaking open like the baby bird's egg, if the egg was five feet three inches tall.

The third eye in Claire's forehead continued to anxiously peer around the room, like it knew something awful was about to happen, but couldn't escape. The high-pitched tone grew louder. Both Tonja and Eve covered their ears and were brought to their knees from the pain caused by the sound. Claire was a hotdog in a microwave, ready to explode. At the height of the piercing noise, Claire's body burst into hundreds of pieces that scattered about the room.

The sound had stopped. Tonja and Eve were absolutely drenched in the viscera that covered the room. Tonja stood up and felt around her shirt for any small, dry space that she could use to wipe the shit out of her eyes. She finally did, and through her blurry, stinging eyes, she looked above the table where Claire had been hanging. There wasn't anything left but a heap of flesh lying on the table.

Tonja turned her attention to Eve. She found a cloth that she used to clean off Eve's face so she, too, could at least open her eyes. They both leaned against the wall to try and come up with some sort of explanation as to what the fuck just happened.

"What the fuck?" Tonja asked.

"Exactly," Eve seconded. "What the fuck?"

"No, I mean, WHAT THE FUCK?"

Eve directed her attention at Tonja, but Tonja was fixated on the heap of flesh on the tabletop. Eve followed her sight line and saw that the heap was moving.

It was a few seconds before they could wrap their heads around what they were seeing. It was a man. A naked man, with his outsides covered in what used to be Claire's insides. He began to stir and sat up on the table's edge, with his hand to his head like he had just woken up with the worst hangover.

Eve's jaw dropped as he lifted his head to reveal his face. It was a face she could never forget.

"Uh...Dad?"

Igor looked up to see his daughter looking at him, just like she did all those years ago, the day he killed himself in front of her.

"Evie?"

"Seriously," Tonja added, "like...what the fuck?!"

# Chapter Eight

# No One Survives – Part I

The Raven's Den was occupied by the usual patrons; the select few that were so graciously allowed to enter. There was a low murmur of conversation and the occasional laughter, but the demons and souls never got too excited unless there was a disagreement, fight, or murder. A few of the tables had games of poker going on, and the bar stools were filled with the drunk and weary, staring longingly into their whiskey, wishing they had some water to quench their eternal thirst.

All the games and conversations came to a screeching halt when the door opened and James, with his crows perched on his shoulders, arms, and head walked through the door.

James was banned from The Den, for no other reason than jealousy. He was "The Chosen One," handpicked by Satan himself. Many of the residents in Oblivion took offense to the fact that he was the one chosen to become The Antichrist, just because he was the grandson of Satan. It was nepotism at its finest.

Lilith was the one who most took exception with Jamie. She was, by all accounts, more than capable of being the Antichrist. Her resume was impeccable, but she, like every other demon, was passed over in favor of James.

Lilith had the respect of everyone in Oblivion and held court within The Den. She was the unofficial authority of who was allowed in, and who received credit. She watched in amusement, with everyone else, as little 'ol Jamie pushed his way between her two lackeys, Damien and Joseph, and bellied up to the bar. The bartender looked at him like he had shit on his lips.

"One whiskey," James demanded.

"Are you a fuckin' idiot, boy?" the bartender responded.

The crowd in the bar went from watching quietly to erupting in laughter. Before Jamie could react to the utter disrespect, Lilith spoke above everyone.

"Everybody, shut the FUCK up!"

An uncomfortable silence swiftly blanketed the place as she walked slowly up to the bar. It was so quiet, the footfalls of her boots could be heard echoing through The Den. James didn't acknowledge her as she forced Damien from his stool so she had room to lean on the bar next to him. James looked forward with both hands on the bar. The crows had dispersed and perched in random spots throughout the bar, watching and waiting.

"Jamie, Jamie, Jamie," Lilith said in a fake, amused tone. "I thought I told you not to come in here again. Did you forget? Or was I not clear?"

James looked up at the bartender, again ignoring Lilith, and said in a calm but forceful tone, "One whiskey. Please."

Lilith laughed and looked around, which made everyone else start laughing. "You think you're a big boy now, Jamie? Or do you think I'll just go away if you ignore me?"

Lilith continued. "You're just a loser like your old man, Jamie. I don't know what Jim ever saw in you. Get the fuck out of my bar before I make you leave, and you find out what happens next, beyond this life."

Lilith grabbed James by the shoulder and turned him. "Fucking look at me when I am talking to you, little boy."

James looked her in the eyes and saw she was serious. But things had changed for Jamie since the last time he was here. He was serious, too.

James pulled away from Lilith's grip and walked behind the bar. Everyone, including Lilith, watched in silence as he poured himself a shot of whiskey, threw it down his throat, and slammed the glass on the counter.

The crowd continued to watch in astonishment as he walked to the back of the room, to an old jukebox that hadn't worked since the beginning of time in Oblivion. He put both hands on top of it and closed his eyes. The lights flickered on and the electricity hummed through the old piece of junk that wasn't even plugged in.

"The music in this shithole has always sucked. Alexa, play *No One Survives*."

*No One Survives* is a brutally amazing song by the metal band Nekrogoblikon. It also features the absolute greatest music video in the history of music videos, and created the perfect vibe for what was about to happen to everyone inside The Raven's Den that day. The non-existent speakers began blaring the song with the opening line:

*Two bill-ion more will die to-night!*

On cue, the crows took flight into the crowd, creating chaos, slashing faces, and clawing at eyes. One crow grabbed Lilith by the hair and ripped out a chunk, along with some bloody scalp. She watched as the bird dropped the bloody clump a few feet away. She calmly walked over and picked it up, and observed in astonishment what unfolded next.

Chris Hingley was sitting closest to the jukebox. He was a demon who was sent to Oblivion because he voiced his opinion against the coup that kicked Jim out of Hell. He would show up at board meetings and make lengthy arguments about the traditional values of Hell. He even started his own group, Make Hell Great Again (MHGA).

James walked up behind Chris, put his hands over both of his ears, and tore his head off his neck. James turned the head around to see the shocked look on Chris' face as he held it up in the air and laughed. Chris' neck spewed blood like a science fair volcano before his body fell out of the chair.

*Imagine stacks of burning flesh!*

*Whole city blocks now house the ashes of mankind!*

Melanie Samson sat across the table from Chris. They had been talking about the good old days of Hell. Melanie never experienced the hell of old, she just listened as he waxed poetic about the good ol' days.

Melanie ended up in Oblivion because, while she was alive, she stood outside her son's school and protested a mask mandate during a global pandemic. She, and a few more stupid fucking hicks from her town, made signs and stood outside the school every morning, in lieu of actually going to work, or contributing something worthwhile to the community. According to Melanie, freedom was more important than keeping her job.

Her son got sick and died from the very disease the mask mandate was trying to protect him from. Melanie got sick as well, and other sick people who weren't assholes got turned away from the hospital because she took up a bed in the ICU. When she woke up, she was in the blistering winds of Oblivion.

Melanie was now drenched in Chris' blood, and wore a similar look of shock on her face. James grabbed her open mouth by the bottom and pulled her jaw down to widen her open mouth even more. He picked up her whiskey glass and slammed it into her mouth, busting out several of her teeth. Blood poured from her gums as James took a step back and front kicked her in the face, shoving the glass further down her gullet while simultaneously breaking her neck. She flew backwards out of the chair and hit the man sitting behind her.

*Sounds of inhuman laughter spreading forth across the earth*

*Look on, there's not much left to see. (Not much at all)*

Theodore Cruise was a fat piece of shit from Texas. He ended up in Oblivion for, well, being a fat piece of shit from Texas. He died while getting gangbanged by the entire United States senate minority and choked on all the ejaculate. The gangbang went on for quite some time before the other members of congress had realized he died.

James broke off a leg from the chair that Melanie had been sitting on and shoved it through the back of Theodore's head. It came out the other side through his mouth.

The blood orgy continued on as Theodore spewed vital fluids onto his buddy Mitchel. Mitchel was an old son of a bitch and his face resembled a miserable turtle. He ended up in Oblivion for a plethora of reasons, but died from a heart attack while ejaculating into Theodore's corpse during the senate gangbang.

James pulled the table leg out through Theodore's mouth and shoved it through Mitchel's eye. He then broke the bottle sitting on the table and slit Mitchel's throat. More blood sprayed across the room. The whole scene made James feel like he was in a Quentin Tarantino movie.

*When all the humans start to die*
*When all that don't shall go insane*
*As they look up at the blackened sky*
*The goblins kill again!*

James, and that whole corner of the bar, was completely soaked in blood. The crows seemed to multiply as they flew through the bar swooping down and attacking indiscriminately. What started out as five birds was now at least ten. The music got louder which caused an adrenaline spike that urged James to continue.

James' eyes had begun to show a white glow, which stood out even more through the crimson mask he now wore. He was on a roll and growing more powerful with each kill.

*In times before the goblins came*
*We only had ourselves to blame*
*For the problems in our lives*
*Spiraling down towards our demise*

Shawn Hassity preached on television and radio against abortions, but forced his mistress to get one. James easily ripped off both of his arms at the shoulders, and he sprayed blood like a fucking fire hydrant. His buddy Carl Tucker was bathing in the blood like a poor kid in the streets of New York on a hot day. James was so powerful now that he swung Shawn's arm like a baseball bat Carl's head and Carl's head exploded. Blood, skull, and brains flew all the way to the farthest side of The Raven's Den.

*We used to laugh, we used to cry*
*Now the only thing we do is die!*
*Dying slowly in the winter light*
*No one survives tonight!*

Pauline Randy sent her son to Catholic school and was proud that he was molested by the priest. She thought he was special for being chosen by a man of God. James punched her in the stomach so hard, his fist put a hole in her. He grabbed her intestines, yanked them out, and then emptied her bowels back into her mouth.

*The end of days is here*
*There is no going back*

Bethany was a bitch, but she didn't deserve to be in Oblivion. She survived some weird shit in her life caused by her unnatural hatred for soup. She was in Oblivion due to a clerical error. Her status was in review when James ripped her in half at the waist.

*The forests burn and the oceans boil*
*The ground is stained forever black*

Teddy Norbit gave ten percent of his income to the NRA and regularly shared articles and videos from Alex Jones on Facebook. James grabbed him by the collar of the shirt with both hands and lifted him into the air before pulling him back down and biting him in the neck. He ripped out a significant chunk of flesh and swallowed it, washing it down with the blood that followed. Teddy screamed as James dropped him to the floor and left him to bleed out.

*The world is gone!*
*A massive grave endures instead*
*Toxic weeds are growing over the bodies of the dead*

Some of the people in the crowd began to run away, but between the birds, confusion, and fear, no one could get anywhere. They stumbled over each other, trampling one another like scared cattle. Lilith was the only one who found a safe spot out of the crowd. She had only suffered one attack from the crows and was watching in awe. She had underestimated James, and she found herself falling in love.

Earl Williams beat his wife and raped his daughter. While he was trying to run away, James grabbed him by the shoulder with his left hand and ripped his spinal cord out of his back with his right hand. Sheila Williams took the beatings from Earl, but also blamed her daughter for Earl raping her. The attention she received had made Sheila jealous. James whipped her across the face with Earl's spinal cord, putting a deep gash in her face. While she was laying on the floor, James rammed the spinal cord up her cunt.

*Whole countries lie ruined*
*Civilization erased*

Drake Wars said that if God wanted his 14-year-old daughter to have that baby, that's what she would do. It didn't matter that it was her 17-year-old brother who raped her. Drake's wife Kathy once told the school board that she didn't want their 8-year-old to wear a mask during the pandemic because she "...wanted the teachers to be able to see her beautiful face." James smashed both of their heads together and they exploded like pumpkins filled with dynamite.

*The oceans infected*
*With nuclear waste*

Dick Barents was a racist piece of shit who said All Lives Matter, but thought it was funny when black kids were shot by cops. James curb-stomped him on a cement ledge below the bar while he was cowering underneath, trying to hide. His head sliced clean off at the jaw.

Roger Zimmer was a cop who shot one of the black kids Dick Barents thought "maybe shouldn't have worn a hooded sweatshirt if he didn't want to get shot thirteen times." He had a "thin blue line" tattoo on his forearm and became a sort of degenerate celebrity when he was acquitted of murder. James put his fingers, which had now grown sharp claws, through Roger's eyes and nose like he was a bowling ball, ripped his head off his neck, and threw it across the room where it landed next to Lilith.

When the music stopped, so did the chaos. Nearly everyone in the Den was dead or dying. Those still clinging to life moaned and groaned and scraped at the floor, pulling themselves towards the door, still trying to escape.

The crows perched up in the rafters and kept an eye on James as he deliberately made his way through the mutilated bodies scattered about the floor, his boots sticking in the blood that covered the ground. He was stalking Lilith.

He had nearly transformed fully into a beast during his killing spree. His eyes were still glowing white, and he bore razor-sharp teeth and claws. His back bulged and bled as his demon wings pushed against his skin, ready to sprout.

He and Lilith now stood face to face. His breath heavy, his body saturated in the blood of Oblivion, but his bloodlust not nearly satiated. Lilith spoke first, her voice trembling.

"I am so fucking wet right now."

James tilted his head slightly but kept his gaze locked on her.

"Seriously, Jamie. I mean, uh, James. Sorry," she stuttered, but gained her composure and started over. "Look, I'm sorry I ever doubted you. How could I have known you had *this* inside you? Think of what we could do together, you and me." Lilith moved forward and bravely put her hands on either side of James' face.

"We could take over the world. We could burn it all to the fucking ground."

For several moments, James didn't make any indication about how he felt. Then, the jukebox kicked back on and played the end of *No One Survives.*

*No one survives the end of the world*
*No one survives the end of the world*

James decapitated her with one swipe of his claw. She never saw it coming. She collapsed to the ground in front of him, her soul joining the rest of Oblivion in whatever came after.

James turned around and looked up at the now uncountable amount of crows that packed The Raven's Den. He raised his hands and whispered, "Feast."

The crows descended in an absolute feeding frenzy and began to devour all those that James had slaughtered. They gorged themselves and picked flesh from the bones until they were clean. They claimed the muscle tissue and the organs. They slurped up every droplet of blood. Every ounce of nourishment fed Jamie and made him stronger. Hours passed until there was nothing left to consume.

James physically returned to looking like himself, but he was not like he was before. He then had a vision, much like the one he saw in his grandfather's eyes. Piles of bodies as far as the eye could see. Him sitting on the throne. God's head on a stake. All was to be as it had been predicted, except for one thing. Jim wasn't next to him on the throne. It was his half-sister, Eve.

James spoke to the crows. "I am the Chosen One. And I will bring about the end. I will travel to Heaven and rid us of the angels. I will fashion a blade from their bones and I will use it to take the head of God herself. I will hold God's head high in triumph as I ride the pale horse across a scorched Earth."

"But first, we will find my sister."

"No one survives the end of the world."

# Chapter Nine

# The Third Trumpet of Revelation

Mary walked into her old room with Pete behind her. It was just as she left it; a fucking mess. It was littered with cigarette butts and empty wine bottles. The television monitors started to kick on, one by one, as she picked up some of the garbage. Pete watched hesitantly, but then started to help her.

Gary was the CEO of the heavenly board. He caught wind of the fact that Mary had returned, and he rushed over to her old room. When he peeked his head in the door and saw her, he meant to scream for security, but Pete saw him and quietly signaled to shut the fuck up. More and more, screens came back online as Mary was engrossed with cleaning up the mess. Pete and Gary peacefully observed, and they became entranced by her.

"I think she's back, Gary," Pete said. "And just in time."

A third trumpet blared and echoed through the heavens.

# Chapter Ten

# I Don't Wanna Go Down to the Basement II

Jim was alone in his new basement setting. It seemed that Kristin hadn't come along on the journey, even though she was the one who had sent him there. He stood up and brushed the concrete dust off his slacks. He looked around at the shitty basement and a smirk appeared on his face. He hadn't seen this place before, but he sure had heard stories about it.

"So this is it;" Jim said aloud to no one, "this is Kristin's famous basement dungeon."

He began to give himself a self-guided tour of the place and point out things he remembered from Kristin's stories.

"Ah, look over there. Her mannequin brains are still splattered on the wall." He closed his eyes and took a big whiff of the air. " I can still smell them, fresh as the day they were blown out of her fucking head."

Jim turned on his heels excitedly and said, "That means...back here must be...yes, there it is!" He had hurried to an adjoining room to see the blood-soaked mattress on the floor. This was where Kristin had cut off Igor's penis and replaced it with a gun.

Jim bent down next to the mattress and pressed on it with his hands. Blood squished out like it had all just happened yesterday. He took it all in and licked his fingers with delight. "What a fuckin' masterpiece this place is."

Jim stood back up and wiped his hands on his clothes. He continued to reminisce out loud. "There was a song, wasn't there? Something about a gun for a dick..."

Jim was interrupted by a thud behind him. He turned around to see a mannequin head rolling on the ground. It came to a stop, with the one good eye looking at him.

"Oh, save the pageantry, Kristin. I'm the fuckin devil for Christ's sake. You've made your point, now let's get the fuck outta here."

Kristin's voice emanated from the mannequin head on the ground, but the lips never moved. Her voice was raspy and distorted. She could only say a few words at a time, like she was having trouble breathing.

"You killed...James...but you think...I will just...let you go? You think...I will just...forget?"

"Kristin, come on." Jim rolled his eyes and was becoming annoyed. "You didn't give a *shit* about that kid. Now all the sudden you're trying to be a good mother? Fuck you, give up the schtick, alright."

Jim looked around the room again. "Hey, how do we get out of here anyway? I've escaped interdimensional prisons before so why can't I find the goddamn door to this shitty basement?"

Kristin's mannequin head started to leak out of the crack over her bad eye. She was crying over the death of her son. However, she would handle her grief the only way she knew how.

The sound of wet flesh slapping against the floor came from the plastic mannequin head. When he looked back at it, he was surprised to see the black, oily tentacles sprouting from the neck. Eight tentacles laced with a thick slime were squirming on the ground. Kristin pulled herself across the floor with the suction cups. The sound was like walking in a wet, muddy field as she made her way to the blood-soaked mattress.

"This...this is new." Jim exclaimed in a cautious tone.

Kristin crawled onto the mattress as her suction cups began slurping the blood from inside. Her mannequin head turned to look directly at Jim as she continued to feed.

Jim regarded her with renewed interest. He loved this kind of shit. He'd been around for an eternity and hadn't seen anything quite like this. He enjoyed Kristin's display as every drop of blood was consumed and the mattress was sucked dry.

"Great trick, Kristin. I mean, really fascinating. I give you all the available points for creativity. But, I really have shit to do..."

For a moment, Jim thought maybe this was the end of the spectacle. Kristin and her tentacles looked inanimate on the mattress, and he couldn't locate any sign of life in her one good eye. He put his hands in his pockets and looked up at the ceiling. Through a sigh, he said, "I really need to find the fucking door."

Kristin's tentacles again began to stir. They started to grow longer and merge together. Jim watched and listened as Kristin's new form began to take shape. Her tentacles began to slap and rub together, combining to resemble human arms and legs. Suction cups became fingers and toes. A nude woman's torso started to take shape. It wasn't long before an almost human-looking woman was standing in front of Jim.

Kristin looked like a person again except for two things. First, her head was still that of a plastic mannequin. The rest of her body appeared to be human flesh, except for the part of her body where her vagina should've been. Instead of a vagina, she had a rock-hard gun for a dick.

"You never cease to amaze me, Kristin, you really don't," Jim said. He took a few steps closer to Kristin until he was face to face with her, and he could feel the cold steel of the cock Glock pressed against his own dick. His tone changed from playfully amused to serious as he put his hand around the barrel and stroked it. "But what the fuck do you think you're gonna do with this?"

When Jim grabbed the gun barrel, he had meant to heat it up until it melted in his hands like steel in a forge, but that didn't happen. As Jim held the ice-cold gun dick, his confidence slowly waned as he realized his powers weren't working. He may be the

Infernal One everywhere else, but in Kristin's basement, he was just another victim.

Kristin tilted her mannequin head to the side as she watched Jim's face contort from bold to fearful. "Oh yeah, Daddy...stroke it FASTER!" Kristin mocked, acting as though she was about to reach orgasm.

It had been a long time since Jim had not been in control of a situation, and a lot longer since he had been scared. You'd have to go back a few millennia to find an instance when Satan was frightened.

Jim opened his mouth to speak, probably to beg or negotiate terms of surrender, but he didn't get a word out as a meaty tentacle filled his mouth and forced its way down his throat. With his eyes wide, he gagged and grabbed at the tentacle as it moved further down his esophagus. The thickness forced his jaw so far open that it popped out of socket.

Kristin shoved him backwards as he choked. She pushed until he was forced up against the wall. She released more tentacles and they wrapped around his ankles. She easily turned him upside down, holding him firmly against the concrete. Four tentacles ripped off all his clothes and then suspended him, two by his ankles and two by his hands. He was spread apart in what looked like a pentagram. A fifth tentacle was still down his throat, and halfway into his stomach. The cold cement bricks in the wall slowly started to heat up.

Jim felt the wall start to get warmer, but didn't register the severity until his back started to sweat. The blocks got progressively hotter until his skin was searing and bubbling like bacon frying in a skillet. He tried to scream, but couldn't with his mouth full. His flesh blistered and eventually melted until he was stuck to the wall without Kristin's additional appendages having to hold him up.

Kristin retracted all her tentacles and Jim let out a torturous scream before catching his breath and sneering at her. "Kristin, you fucking bitch! You can't do this to ME! Do you know what will happen to you when I finally get out of here? It will be the end of you. I guarantee whatever you do to me here, I will do so much fucking worse."

"We will have to see about that, won't we Jim?"

# Chapter Eleven

# The Castration of Satan

Kristin stood in front of Jim as he hung upside down, stuck to the wall by his melted flesh. She let loose one of her tentacles to open a closet door. Inside was an old CRT television that sat on the top shelf of a wheeled cart. Kristin's tentacle wrapped around the cart and pulled it towards her.

The second shelf of the cart had a VCR and with a VHS tape sitting on top of it. The tape looked like it had been recorded over several times. The titles on the label had been crossed off and re-written. The video tape was originally *Joey's 3rd Grade Musical,* and then someone accidentally recorded over it with a partial episode of MTV's *Total Request Live.* After Joey recorded some softcore porn from Cinemax over the rest of the tape, it was reused once again and labeled *Castration Instructional with Farmer Tim Gilbert*.

Kristin let Jim read the title before she put the VHS cassette in the VCR. She clicked on the TV and then pressed play. The picture was blurred by hundreds of horizontal lines.

"Fuck, this VCR doesn't even have auto tracking? What kind of budget am I dealing with here? Hold on, Jim, I have to adjust this real quick. I know, it really ruins the aesthetic I'm going for here. But don't worry, we will get it back."

"Ah, there we go!"

The picture was black and white and showed Farmer Tim. He was wearing his overalls over his flannel shirt, standing awkwardly in front of the camera while several piglets ran around his feet, making all kinds of commotion. Tim stared directly into the camera, clearly uncomfortable.

The narrator sounded like he was the disembodied off screen voice that would talk to old cartoon characters.

Narrator: Hey there, Farmer Tim! Say hello to the audience.

Tim's nerves made him forget how to blink, and slowly raised his hand to wave "Hello" into the camera.

Narrator: Okay... Well, today, Farmer Tim is going to demonstrate how to castrate a piglet. Are you ready to begin, Tim?

Tim: Uh...Yup.

Tim barely opened his mouth when he talked and spoke out of the left side, so it was sort of hard to understand what he had to say. He was there less for his dialogue and more for the demonstration.

Narrator: As Farmer Tim wrangles a piglet, how about a little bit of history behind the castration of swine? For example, did you know that the vast majority of male piglets are castrated?

Kristin was watching the screen intently. "Oh, Jim, I didn't know that. Did you know that? I wonder, why?"

Narrator: Why, you ask?

Kristin perked up and laughed. "Hey, did you hear that, Jim? It's like he heard me."

Narrator: Well, castration is performed to avoid boar taint in the meat of sexually mature male pigs, and to reduce aggression toward other pigs and caretakers. Boar taint is an accumulation of compounds, such as skatole and androstenone, in the meat of intact males that causes unpleasant smells and tastes to be released when the pork is heated.

"Well that just sounds gross, doesn't it, Jim? We can't have unpleasant tasting bacon. Oh, and intact males means males that still have their balls, Jim. Just in case you were wondering."

Narrator: Well, it looks like Farmer Tim was able to secure us a piglet. Are you ready to move forward, Tim?

Tim raised the squealing piglet by the hind legs and smiled a half smile. He gave a thumbs up, signaling he was ready to continue.

Jim watched Kristin, in both shock and terror, as she gathered the few tools she needed for the upcoming job. He tried to plead with her one more time, but Kristin extended a tentacle that shot back down his throat to prevent him from speaking.

"Shh, Jim. You wouldn't want to distract me, would you? I'd hate to fuck this up."

"Now, we can't do anything about your unpleasant smell. You've had your balls way too long for that. I could smell the androstenone the minute your flesh started searing against the wall. But you killed my son, and now I'm going to treat you like the fucking swine you are."

Narrator: Currently there are two methods of castrating male piglets: surgical castration and immunocastration. Today, Farmer Tim will be demonstrating surgical castration. Tim, would you like to take it from here?

Tim: Uh...sure. So, uh, first ya gotta hang 'em upside down, ya know. I, I used to hang 'em over there, but the daggum board broke. So, I, uh, I went to the wife and I said honey, I'm gonna need to use the X-cross up in our bedroom to cut the pig balls today. Well, she got all up in a hissy fit, ya know how women git. She likes it when I use the X-cross to tie 'er up in the rope and hang 'er upside down at night before we get to baby makin'.

Tim: Anyway, I borrowed our X-cross so we can cut the balls off this here piggy. Now, it gets pretty bloody. But trust me, this ain't the first time this contraption has seen some blood, if you know what I mean.

Kristin looked down at Jim. "Turns out old Farmer Tim isn't as shy as we thought, eh?"

Tim: So what you do is you string the little piggy up like so. Now he's gonna scream at ya, but ya can't blame the poor little guy. The sumbitch is gettin' his balls lopped off, for Christ's sake.

Narrator: Castration is typically performed without anesthesia. However, surgical castration involves cutting and manipulating innervated tissue, and if anesthesia is not provided, it will be painful for the animal.

Kristin knelt down and put her plastic face against Jim's. "There will be plenty of blood, Jim. I want to hear you squeal for me. Squeal like the little piglet you are, it makes my steel dick even harder when you squeal."

Narrator: Watch Farmer Tim as he makes sure the piglet is secure. He will either make two vertical cuts or one horizontal cut to the skin of the scrotum. It looks like he's using the vertical cut method. Now that he's done the cutting, the testes are removed by cutting the spermatic cord with a scalpel or pulling until the cord tears.

Tim yanked on the spermatic cord as the piglet squealed and squealed in agony. Farmer Tim's bloody hand held up the testicles for the camera to see. He now had a full smile across his face.

"I guess it's our turn, Jimbo"

Jim tried to scream, but it was only a muffled whimper through the tentacle in his throat. Blood poured from Jim's scrotum, down his torso, and over his face. Kristin bent down close, with both of his testicles in her hand, so he could get a really good look.

"I nicked you, Jim. I tried pulling until the cord tore, but you have some tough spermatic cord, so I had to use a knife. You might bleed out right here, but I sure hope not. I am far from done."

# Chapter Twelve

# The Bitchification of Satan

Jim hung upside down on that wall for five days. He lost a lot of blood, but he didn't die. Kristin had left just moments after removing his testicles. She left his balls on the floor where he could see them, and hadn't returned since.

Jim lost so much more than just blood over those five days. He had never been this powerless in all his existence. He didn't even know it was possible to be this helpless. On day three, he even resorted to praying to his former lover and baby momma, God. Mary, like she did to everyone else, never responded.

On day five, Jim was just another human being begging for death. He cried and called out through his dry throat and swollen tongue for Kristin to end his life. Finally, he opened his eyes and saw a dick gun hanging in front of him.

"It only took five days to turn Lucifer into a full-on bitch, huh? Five fuckin days and the loss of your balls, I guess. Still, I would have thought you'd lasted longer than that, but such is the fragile male ego. So it goes."

Kristin squatted down so her one good mannequin eye made contact with Jim's. "You're not just a bitch, Jim. You're a special bitch. You're my bitch. And you're also a modern scientific miracle! In the five days you've spent without your balls, you've become such a bitch that you've developed a female reproductive system. That's right, I can see it. You've got a fucking uterus, fallopian tubes, the whole fucking works. Absolutely amazing."

Jim couldn't speak. He couldn't even comprehend what Kristin was saying. He was dehydrated and barely conscious.

"Making men my bitch has been my forte over the years, Jim. And it seems I've reached the pinnacle of my accomplishments. I have made Satan my bitch. Wow. Can you believe it?"

Kristin stood up and unleashed her tentacles once again. This time she gripped Jim and pulled him off the wall. He screamed as his flesh ripped from the wall. He laid on his stomach, revealing his raw and bloody back. Kristin pulled him up by the back of the neck and bent him over a nearby table. The same table she had sat on when Igor blew her brains out with his dick gun.

Kristin used a tentacle to go up Jim's ass and root around. "Just as I suspected from a bitch like you. Your asshole is also your vagina. Jesus Christ, I am so fucking horny right now."

Without any further warning, Kristin shoved her cock Glock in Jim's asshole. He screamed in agony initially, but then tried his best to stay silent. With each thrust, Kristin thought back to how she used to pound Igor with her strap-on dildo, but that was crunchy peanut butter compared to what she was doing now. This was the big time. Jim deserved this for murdering her son. And she had just conquered the fucking Devil, for Christ's sake.

As Kristin thrusted inside Jim, she began to sing Igor's song. The last time she heard it, it didn't end well for her, but she felt it was appropriate now. With each thrust, she would sing the next line.

*I've*

*Got a gun*

*For a dick*

*A dick gun*

*Yes, I've*

*got a gun*

*For a dick*

*A dick gun*

*I've got a Glock*

*For my cock*

*I've got a gat*

*For my prick*

*A gun for my DIIIIIIIICK*

*Dick Gun.*

When Kristin reached "a gun for my diiiiiiick," she blew her gunshot cumshot into Jim. The money shot was loud, muffled slightly from being so deep inside him. She bent herself over his raw, skinless back and kissed him on the neck. She then whispered the final line of the song into his ear. "Dick Gun, bitch."

And then she disappeared, leaving Jim to bleed from his ravaged asshole.

# Chapter Thirteen

# Ass Baby

Eight months had gone by since Jim had seen Kristin. His belly looked like it was about to pop. He had gone through a lot physically and emotionally over those eight months.

Jim's wounds never healed, they stayed as raw as the day he received them. His back never grew any new skin. His asshole was as devastated as the day the dick gun had been mercilessly shoved inside him. He hadn't had a drink of water or a morsel of food.

It took a few months for Jim to actually accept he was pregnant. Despite all the shit he had been through, in all his existence, in which the length of time was really unknowable, he didn't believe he could really carry a child in his male body. But once his baby bump started to show, he had to accept it.

Even though he was malnourished, the baby inside him was thriving and growing. In his isolation, he started talking to his baby. It was the only company he had, and as time went on, he began to love his unborn child. Not only love him or her, but also cherish the idea of being a mommy. He worried that he would give birth in the dirty basement all alone and the baby wouldn't survive. But if it did, he would do his best to take care of it. He hoped Kristin would show up again, so he could convince her to let him take care of their child outside of the basement.

He decided, boy or girl, he would name the baby Remington. Remi for short.

***

Nearly nine months had passed when Jim could feel Remi was on her way. He hadn't been sure how this was going to work, but he felt like he really had to poop. Since he hadn't eaten in eight months, he figured that was how Remi was going to introduce herself.

After sixteen hours of labor, Remi pushed her way out of Satan's rectum. Up until now,

Kristin hadn't come back, so Jim was worried about how he would nourish his baby. He looked down at his newly formed bitch tits and thought he would try nursing. That's when Kristin came back.

"Oh, look at this! You're a mommy! Does that make me a daddy? Hmm, I don't know, this is all very confusing."

"Kristin, please. Look, we have a baby together now. We can make this work. Please. I'm sorry about James. But Remi can be a new start for the both of us. Just take us out of here."

"Holy shit, Jim, you really are a bitch now aren't you? I'm not fucking taking you or this bastard baby anywhere."

"Then can you just leave us here? Give me what I need to take care of her. Please? I'm begging you!"

"Yeah, I'm well aware that you're begging. But I'm not here to take care of that ass baby. I'm here to make you feel like you made me feel when you killed my fucking son."

Jim looked at Kristin in absolute horror. "No, Kristin. Please. I'll do anything. Don't hurt her!" He began crying.

Kristin moved slowly towards Jim while she talked, and then kneeled down in front of him.

"To paraphrase the great Mike Tyson; 'I'm the best ever. I'm the most brutal and vicious, the most ruthless there's ever been. There's no one that can stop me. There's no one like me. There's no one that can match me. I'm just ferocious. I want your heart. I want to eat your fucking children.'"

Jim continued to look at Kristin with panic and confusion. "What? You want to...what?

"I'm going to eat that fucking ass baby of yours, Jim. Fuck you."

Kristin's mannequin mouth opened for the first time. It opened wide like a snake with razor-sharp teeth. She once again released her tentacles and went to grab baby Remington from Jim's arms. Jim screamed, "Please, no!" when suddenly there was a flash of white, and the basement was empty.

# Chapter Fourteen

# Hard to Find

George was back at it. He had his protective gear on and was manning the controls through the earthquake. He was The Grinderman once again. He didn't know whose soul was coming. Could it be Igor? *It couldn't be*, he thought. *There was nothing left of his soul. Rosemary said so...*

George was brought back to the present as the thud of a soul crashed upon the platform. George could see it was that of a young woman. She was flailing and crying out, much like Igor used to do. George couldn't hear what she was saying over the roaring of the machine, but he did like he always had and pulled the first lever. The platform tilted forward, and the soul slid onto the conveyor belt. George pulled the second lever to start the conveyor, and finally the third to start the blades.

George watched as this new soul continued to scream and cry in fear, presumably begging him to stop. But he didn't stop the machine, and the soul of the young woman was shredded by the blades.

George stood at the end of the machine waiting for the ground-up pieces to fill the basket. He shut the machine down, removed his welder's helmet and protective suit, and took the basket of torn soul remains to Rosemary.

"Do you know who it is? Is it Thomas?" asked Rosemary. She preferred Thomas over Igor.

"It was a young lady, as far as I could tell."

Rosemary reached in the basket and started feeling the pieces of soul she had to work with. She opened her mouth wide in surprise and looked at George.

"Georgie...It's...It's her."

George put his hand over his mouth and spoke through it. "We've read so much about her. And now she's here?"

"She is here. Let me get to work so we can finally meet Evie."

George sat on the couch in the living room with nervous anticipation. When Igor would come visit, he would write everything he could remember in journals. The longest, most heartbreaking entry was about his daughter Evelyn, or as he called her, Evie.

George and Rosemary had read that journal too many times to count. Just as they grew to love Igor as a son, they would think of Evelyn as their granddaughter. Though they had never met her, they knew they loved her.

While George waited, he went to the study where Igor used to write. He took the journal from the top of the stack and went back to the living room. He opened it up to his favorite passage Igor had written about his little Evie. What broke his heart most was that Igor wrote it in the present tense. Igor hadn't fully grasped that he would never see his baby girl ever again.

*Evie is such a daddy's girl, but more importantly than that, I am this amazing little girl's daddy. I can still feel the weight of her as she hugs my arm when we are standing close. She hugs me so tight, for seemingly no reason, and I can lift my arm and swing her around in circles. I never want to forget the sound of her laughter. I never want to forget that look of love and complete trust in her eyes.*

*Evie can't go to bed without me tucking her in, and frankly I never want her to. I'll tuck her in as long as she will let me. Her mother says I baby her too much, but I don't care. I'll sit by her bed and she and I will write bedtime songs and make up our own bedtime stories.*

*The song we came up with is so cheesy, but it's ours. We even have our own hand motions to go along with it. God, if there is a God, don't let me forget the lyrics.*

*Evie, the moon is out tonight*
*Evie, the stars are shining bright*
*Evie, it's time to close your eyes*
*Evie, it's time to say goodnight*
*And I'll see you, in the morning*

*When the sun is in the sky*

*And I'll see you, in the morning*

*When you open up your eyes*

*Evie, the day is done*

*Evie, the day has turned to night*

*Evie, Daddy loves you so much*

*Evie, it's time to say goodnight.*

*We sing this song together and she won't let me leave until I wrap her in blankets like a burrito. There has to be a way back to her.*

George had just finished reading and wiped the tears from his eyes, when the door to Rosemary's room opened and she walked out with Evelyn. Rosemary was behind her with her hand on her shoulder, leading her out.

"George, I'd like you to formally meet Evelyn."

George stood and walked forward a few steps. Without saying anything, he embraced her. Evelyn was stiff in his arms for a few moments before she returned the embrace. She couldn't remember another time in her life that she felt so safe and so loved. After a few moments, Rosemary spoke.

"We never know how much time you have here. I'm sure you have so many questions. Your father always did."

Evelyn released her hug from George and looked at Rosemary.

"My dad has been here before?"

"Oh yes, more times than we count. We loved him like he was our own son. And we learned so much about you as a little girl. We always thought of you as our granddaughter."

"I'm so confused. Can you tell me why I'm here? Can you tell me anything about my dad?"

Rosemary answered as George put his arm around Evelyn's shoulders. "I don't know why you are here, honey. And I think the best way for you to learn about your father is straight from the horse's mouth."

George led Evelyn to the study where Igor used to write in his journals. Rosemary followed close behind. Both she and George stopped at the doorway and watched Evelyn as she approached the desk. She timidly sat down in the desk chair and reached for a book.

"Oh wait," George interrupted, "start with this one." He handed her the journal he had just been reading. "It's our favorite."

From then on, Evelyn never looked up from the journals. She read every story from every life that her father lived. Every horrible story from his relationship with Kristin, to his infatuation with a luchador, and learned more about the fact that he was the son of God and Satan.

George periodically checked on her as she read and kept her glass full of iced tea. Soon, he noticed she was beginning to fade.

"I think it's almost time for you to go, Evie."

She closed the book she was reading and looked up. "Where am I going?"

Rosemary came back into the room now and stood with George. "We don't know," said Rosemary. "We never know when you're leaving, where you're going, or if we will ever see you again."

"Can I just stay here? I don't want to go back. I just want to stay here with you two."

"We'd love for you to stay!" Rosemary exclaimed as she grabbed George's hand. "But we don't make the rules. Just know we love you. I hope you're able to remember that. We love you. And your father loved you, too."

Before Evelyn could respond, she was gone. When she opened her eyes again, she was in the back seat of Cash's car having a coughing fit. She took a drink from a bottle of water that Tonja had given her and said, "Surprise."

# Chapter Fifteen

# Where Is Her Head?

Eve, Tonja, and Igor were all covered in the blood and guts of Claire, the latest victim in the legacy of Rotten. Eve looked at her newly emerged and naked father as he sat on the table, unable to speak.

"Evie, is that you?"

Eve took two steps back, shook her head, and ran out into the parking lot.

Igor stood up and then looked at Tonja with sudden recognition. "Tonja? What is going on here?"

"Well that's something we'd all like to know, now isn't it? I'm going to check on your daughter. Find something to cover your dick and meet me outside."

Tonja found Eve outside by the car. She was bent over with her hands on her knees, crying. She was standing over a pile of fresh vomit.

"Eve. Are you okay?"

Tonja put her hand on Eve's back. Eve couldn't respond; she could only cry and dry heave. Behind them, Igor came out of the station wrapped in a towel. If anyone drove by, they were in for a sight.

"Do you need some of your medicine?" Tonja asked.

"What kind of medicine does she need?" Igor questioned.

Tonja looked up at Igor and then got in his face. "She hooked on fucking heroin, no thanks to you."

Igor's heart dropped. He had been back on this Earthly plane for all of ten minutes and his guilt just caught up to him.

"Evie, I'm so sorry. What can I do to----?"

"Don't fucking call me that!" Eve interrupted. She had stood up and looked at her father.

"They said I'd forget," Eve continued. "They said I would forget everything I learned, but I didn't forget."

Neither Tonja nor Igor knew what Eve was talking about. A couple crows started circling overhead.

Tonja said, "Look, I think you might just need a little medicine to calm you down." She started toward the car to grab the bag.

"I don't need any fucking medicine," Eve said through her clenched teeth. She returned her focus to Igor.

"I met George and Rosemary, Dad. I read all your journals. They said I would forget but I didn't forget. I remember everything."

"You...you died? And you ended up there, in Armageddon?"

"I did. George and Rosemary, they loved you like a son. And they love me. More than I can say for anyone else I've ever met in my life."

"Hold on," Igor responded, "that's not fair."

"Not fair? Not FAIR? How many chances do you get?"

Igor squinted at Eve questioningly, not quite following.

"How many chances do you get to get it right, Dad? You died and came back to life how many times? It's truly unknowable. Your parents are GOD and THE FUCKING DEVIL! Yet look at all those lives, all those chances, and all that potential you wasted."

Eve's voice got stronger and louder as she continued. She walked slowly toward Igor. Tonja stood by watching this all happen, noticing the changes in the surroundings. The wind had picked up and more crows began riding in on the air current.

"You had two children. Two! Two lives that you brought into this world that you left behind. You couldn't just fuck up your own lives, one after another, you had to fuck us up, too. Here I am, a fucking dope fiend because my mother, your wife, shot me up for the first time."

"And what about your son? Where is he? What happened, or is happening to him right now?"

Igor watched as something inside Evelyn changed. He didn't know exactly what was happening to her, but he knew it wasn't good. He backed up from Eve, trying to come up with words to make things make sense. But there weren't any words.

The wind was blowing so hard now that the dust was tearing at their skin. Tonja ducked into the driver's side of the car to get out of it. She watched the altercation between Igor and Eve continue to escalate and realized that maybe this was beyond her now. Tonja, ever the survivor, started the car and slammed her foot down on the gas pedal. Igor looked away from Evelyn, for only a moment, to see the taillights disappear in the foreboding darkness that approached.

Something hit Igor in the face, and it hit him hard. Before he could comprehend what just happened, something else hit him in the chest and he fell to the ground, losing his towel.

The wind was blowing fast, and the crows rode the air currents like speeding bullets. It was a couple of those crows that had hit Igor and knocked him down. Before he knew it, thousands were speeding towards him, blocking out any sight he had of Evelyn. He tried to stand, but was cut by beaks and claws and collapsed again.

Suddenly, the wind stopped. What seemed to be an infinite number of crows now calmly circled the skies, awaiting instructions. Next to Evelyn stood Igor's son, and Evelyn's brother, James.

Igor stood up and looked at his two children, with his dong flopping in what was now a gentle breeze.

James spoke first. "Jesus Christ. Look at you two, covered in blood and tears and puke. And good old Dad over there with his dick out in front of his kids."

Igor covered himself with one hand and started to say something but James interrupted. “Hey. No onc needs to hear from you, okay? You had your time. You had your chances. I don’t know how you got back here, *again*, but no one wants you here. Fuck off on your own free will, or I’ll make you.”

The crows came down in a cloud around Igor as he tried to swat them away. He looked again at Evelyn and James like he wanted to say something.

“I won’t say it again, Igor. Fuck off.”

Igor looked longingly at his children, but turned and started walking away with the crows ushering him down yet another path of shame.

James and Evelyn stood face to face. James spoke first.

“I’ve been keeping an eye on you for a while, and now I’ve finally found you.”

“I thought you’d be taller,” Evelyn responded.

“What?”

“And you look like you’re 20 years older than me. What the hell happened to you?”

“This isn’t exactly how I thought meeting my sister for the first time would go.”

“It’s not quite what I expected either. Or you would have been taller and younger-looking..”

James looked at her in disbelief.

“Oh, come on James, I’m fucking with you. Are you always so serious?”

"Things have been pretty serious for me lately, so yeah, kinda."

"Great, well, we'll work on that. What are we going to do now?"

"You and I will reign supreme over Heaven, Hell, and Earth. We will sit among towers of corpses on thrones constructed with the bones of the angels. We will bring everything as we know it to an end."

"So serious. So dramatic," Eve said sarcastically. But as she looked into James's glowing eyes, she became lost in them.

In his eyes, she saw the pestilence James meant to bring upon the world. She felt the pain of each person suffering through a Godless apocalypse, and it was an all too familiar feeling. Eve looked inside herself for her empathy, but found none. Not one single person had given a shit about her up until now. Not her parents, not her teachers, not a single motherfucker on this plane of existence. To her, this world and all the people in it, wasn't worth saving.

In every story Eve ever read, or television show she ever watched, there was always a pure and righteous character to fight against evil. There was one person with an unwavering moral compass that put everything on the line for the greater good. But this wasn't a book or a show, this was real life. And in real life, there are no heroes. None that she had ever met.

"What do you say?" James asked, bringing her back.

"I'm in. Let's fuck this shit up."

# Chapter Sixteen

# The Fourth Trumpet of Revelation

Mary leaned forward with her hands on the sink of her bathroom and looked into the mirror of the medicine cabinet. She looked into her own eyes for the first time in a long, long time. She turned on the cold sink water and splashed her face when the fourth trumpet sounded. She opened the cabinet and got her toothbrush and toothpaste, and began brushing her teeth.

# Chapter Seventeen

# No One Survives – Part II

Evelyn and James found themselves back in Northwest Ohio. They both figured the best place to begin the Apocalypse was at home, where their story began. Their first stop was at The Church of the Cross. Eve said they should start there because they always had dumbass signs outside with ridiculous sayings. On that day, the sign read: "*IF PRAYING WAS A FULL-TIME JOB, WOULD YOU STILL BE EMPLOYED?*"

They stood outside the doors of the church on a Sunday morning. They were side by side when Eve looked over at James. He had his eyes closed and was taking deep breaths. His crows circled the sky above them, awaiting command.

"Are you good?" asked Eve.

"Oh, I'm good," James responded. "I'm just preparing. Every great film has a great soundtrack."

***

Bowling 4 Jesus was a southern gospel acapella quartet as well as an amateur bowling team. The four men in the group wore matching bowling shirts and khakis. On the back of their bowling shirts, there was an illustration of Jesus Christ holding a bowling ball with a yellowish glow around it. Jesus seemed to be deep in concentration, possibly looking to pick up a spare. They stood in front of the congregation of The Church of the Cross, singing in their signature harmony the Sunday morning opener, *Sing to Me of Heaven.*

*Sing to me of Heaven, sing that song of peace*
*From the toils that bind me, it will bring release*
*Burdens will be lifted that are pressing so*
*Showers of great blessing o'er my heart will flow*

Pastor Eugene Robinson stood in the back, waiting for the cue to make his grand entrance. He peeked through the curtain at the supple young girl in the front row and licked the sweat from above his top lip.

The air conditioning in the church was broken, and some of the people in the pews were waving their faces with the pamphlets the pastor's helper passed out, trying to cool down. The pamphlet was titled with the subject of the days sermon, *Punishment & Judgement.*

Bowling 4 Jesus finished their song and the tenor, Billy, stepped forward to introduce Pastor Eugene. Eugene was caught off guard, as he was fixated on eleven-year-old Sadie McGowan. It was a good thing he had on loose robes to hide his hard dick.

The pastor walked out smiling and waving, took his place at the podium, and adjusted the microphone. It made a loud screech that echoed through the church and made some of the people cringe.

"Well, I'd say it's hotter than hell in here, but we all know that's not true." Eugene gave one awkward chuckle at his own joke, but stopped when no one else laughed. There was only a dry cough from the back, and the rustling of a few people who were adjusting the way they were sitting. They all just wanted this to be over with.

Pastor Eugene wanted this to be over with, too. He had a hell of a hangover.

"Speaking of hell, let's talk about hell today."

Eugene cleared his throat and began.

"The Bible clearly teaches us that hell is real. Every New Testament author mentions it. You have Matthew.

And Mark.

Luke.

John.

Um, you also have Paul.

James.

Peter.

Uh, who am I missing? Oh, right, Jude.

And, uh, whoever wrote Hebrews..."

Eugene began trailing off and stopped to dab his forehead with his handkerchief. He cleared his throat and walked to the side of his podium, trying to ignore the seductive gaze of little Sadie.

"The point is, we all have to take hell seriously. And if we start reading what the Bible has to say about hell, one of the things we'll quickly notice is that the authors use different images to describe its reality.

Punishment.

Destruction.

And as your pamphlet states, Exile.

Each of these descriptions teaches us something different about nature of hell."

"Let's first talk about punishment. Punishment, you see, is the, uh, the main way the Bible describes hell, and it is usually portrayed in three different ways.

Judgment.

Suffering.

And torment by fire."

*And maybe a bit of spanking for the bad little girl in the front row...*

Pastor Eugene was so boring, congregation member Richard Graves thought maybe this was his own personal hell. *I'd rather be tormented by fire than hear you say another fucking word, pastor.*

"In Matthew 25, Jesus claims the authority as the judge who determines the destinies of the world. He consigns the wicked to eternal punishment and grants the righteous eternal *life*."

At least a few of the people in the congregation were starting to get into the spirit of Eugene's words and said, "Amen!" when he mentioned the righteous being granted eternal life. Eugene appreciated that and started putting some more energy into his speech.

"Jesus again in Mark 9:43-48, speaking of the seriousness of sin, says these words, 'If your hand causes you to sin, cut it off. It is better for you to enter life crippled than to have two hands and go into hell. Into the unquenchable fire.

He continued, "And if your eye causes you to sin, pluck it out. It is better for you to enter the kingdom of God with one eye than to have two eyes and be thrown into hell, where their worm never dies, and the fire is never quenched!'"

"Amen!"

"Yes, Sir!"

"Praise Him!"

Eugene picked up the pace once again. "The apostle John, in Revelation 20, says 'We see the wicked are cast into the lake of fire, while the righteous experience the unhindered and glorious presence of God on the New Earth!"

"Hallelujah!"

The entire audience had now forgotten how hot they were. A few of them stood up and put their hands in the air, like they were waiting for God's embrace. Others were hooting and hollering like their favorite football team just scored a touchdown. "Amens" continued to scatter throughout the church. If they only knew that on most Sundays, God was sleeping off a bender and not paying any mind to them or their meaningless lives.

Eugene had the people in the palm of his hand, and thought maybe now was a good time to segue into all the passages of the good book that alluded to the practice of men fucking young children. *If it was good enough in biblical times, why wouldn't it be good enough today? Should we really let modern society dictate morality, when it's all laid out in the word of God?* He was still contemplating the idea when he was interrupted.

The front doors opened and the sunlight that came through blinded Pastor Eugene. He could only see the silhouettes of James and Evelyn standing in the doorway. Everyone in the church had also turned around, shielding their eyes, trying to see who was late to church today so they could shame them later.

"Uh, thanks for coming, you two," Eugene said, "but could you come in and shut the door? I'm sure one of your fellow members can get you caught up on what we are talking about today."

"We are all caught up," said Eve. "We are here to judge. We are here to sentence the wicked."

James spoke next. "And the judgment is this: *NO ONE SURVIVES.*"

On cue, the crows flew in through the doors, causing immediate mayhem. At the same time, music started blaring from seemingly nowhere, and Nekrogoblikon once again proclaimed:

*Two bill-ion more will die to-night!*

Ursula was sitting in the back of the church. She had only recently found the lord, but she felt in her heart that she owed God her life.

Ursula couldn't help but be drawn to the most toxic of men, and one bad date with a man she had met on the internet nearly ended her life. The man who called himself Eric had taken her back to his house. Except it wasn't his house, it was a newly built house in a brand new subdivision. Another house was being built behind that one, waiting for the foundation to be poured.

Eric beat the shit out of Ursula until she was unconscious, and then threw her in the hole waiting to be filled with concrete. When she woke up, she was already being covered. The concrete rose higher as she started to become aware of what was happening. Eric's concrete mixer growled loudly, drowning out any attempt Ursula had made at screams for help.

Ursula couldn't fight the weight of the wet concrete as it crept closer to covering her mouth. She was only saved when the concrete mixer ground to a halt. Frustrated, Eric went to troubleshoot what the fuck was wrong with his machine. Something popped and the mixer, which was tipped forward pouring the concrete, came crashing down and crushed Eric beneath.

It was a shame that Ursula had survived such a tragedy, only to be the first one killed in the beginning of the apocalypse. Eve had pulled a heavy metal cross off the wall that depicted Jesus being crucified, came up behind Ursula, and swung it so Jesus's left arm busted through her right eye socket.

Ursula's blood sprayed all over Janice, an elderly woman whose husband passed away two years ago. *Finally,* she thought, after she had poisoned his breakfast for the six months prior. Eve had ripped the cross from Ursula's skull and used it to bash Janice's face. She bludgeoned Janice three times, turning her face to hamburger, making her completely unrecognizable.

Meanwhile, the crows attacked the congregation, continuing to create chaos while Evelyn and James worked. James came up behind Dillan and Lindsey Perry. They had just had a beautiful baby boy together. Well, Dillan had suspicions about his wife when the baby came out looking like a different ethnicity than either him or Lindsay. He would never know if he was really the father or not because James grabbed them both by the hair and simultaneously yanked their heads back so hard, their necks broke over the back of the pews. Their spines splintered and poked through the front of their necks.

Richard Graves was a fat son of a bitch who could barely fit in the pew. He always had a piece of food stuck to his face. Eve finished up with the cross when she straddled him and shoved it down his throat, piercing through the base of his skull.

Jeremy Pierce prayed every night, asking God to help him get the promotion he deserved. Robert had been given the promotion, but he was a kiss-ass and wasn't half as good as Jeremy. Jeremy would daydream about walking the corridors of the office, when the CEO would see him, and instantly recognize his potential. The boss would pull him close, lay Jeremy's head on his shoulder, and whisper in his ear, "Son, I've been hearing good things." Jeremy would then look into Robert's corner office and give him double-fisted middle fingers.

Jeremy was once again praying that he would be spared and Robert would be killed, when James ripped his heart from his chest and held it over his head, letting the blood flow and drip in and around his mouth.

Robert Flake really was an arrogant asshole who believed his own bullshit. He thought for a split second he could negotiate a deal to save his life. Eve lifted him up like a feather and brought him down across her knee, breaking him in half.

Frank hadn't moved amongst all the chaos. In fact, he wasn't really sure how he even ended up in the church. Hell, he wasn't totally convinced he was in the church at all. He was wearing a bathrobe over his pajamas and had taken a copious amount of LSD for breakfast. He thought this was all a trip and was smiling at how crazy this all was when James grabbed him and threw him like a ragdoll through the stained glass window. He went through the windshield of Robert's BMW in the parking lot.

Pastor Eugene couldn't believe his eyes. His entire congregation was being murdered before him. He watched the birds feed on their bodies, efficiently picking them clean until there was nothing left but bones.

Eugene made his way down the stage stairs to grab a terrified Sadie McGowan's hand. He got to her just as Evelyn was ripping her mother's eyes from her skull. He pulled her back up the stairs and tried to run for the back door, but was stopped by a flurry of crows.

James and Evelyn were now in front of Pastor Eugene, slowly making their way up the few steps that led up to his platform. James had turned from human to hellish beast. His large, black wings had once again burst through the skin of his back. He bore his razor teeth and claws at pastor Eugene.

Evelyn was glowing with power. She wasn't shapeshifting like James, but her skin radiated bright orange light, and she had gained immense strength throughout the killing spree. She felt an endless thirst for blood and suffering.

Everyone else in the church had been killed. Eugene pushed Sadie behind him and clutched the cross that hung around his neck. He prayed out loud, asking Jesus for forgiveness, one last time.

"I know who God is," said James, "and she isn't listening."

Eugene forgot for a second that he was about to die and got a puzzled look on his face. "She?"

"Are you fucking kidding me?" Evelyn asked, right before she grabbed his hair and ripped his head clean off his shoulders. Blood spewed from his neck and showered little Sadie McGowan.

Evelyn held the pastor's head in her hands as she bent down and looked Sadie in the eyes. Sadie was so terrified she couldn't even cry. She had, however, pissed her pants.

"Listen, girl. The deal is that no one survives. And to be honest, you aren't going to. You are going to die very soon because no one survives the end of the world. But, I have a soft spot for girls like you. I'm letting you walk out of here today, but I'm sure I'll see you again. Soon."

Fifteen minutes later, they walked out of the church, their aura's glowing a bright white, and Evelyn still carrying the pastor's head by the hair.

"Should we give them a chance to surrender in the future?" Evelyn wondered out loud to James.

"Why would we do that?"

"Well, I'm just thinking that if we kill everyone, who is going to do all the work? We need some slaves, ya know?"

"Ugh. What a pain in the ass that's going to be...but I think you're right."

A city police car drove by and slowed down. He had never seen that many black birds in his life. He was watching them fly in circles above the church when he noticed the pair just having a casual conversation, even though they were covered in blood, and the woman was carrying what seemed to be a man's head. "What in the fuck?" he said in disbelief, before flipping on his lights and stopping in front of them. He got out of the police car and pulled his gun.

"You two, get on the ground!"

Evelyn and James both nonchalantly took notice.

"Fuck you, man," Evelyn said. "Can't you see we are trying to have a conversation?" She raised both arms in the air in annoyance, the pastor's head swinging from her hand.

Before the police officer could say anything else, Evelyn had whipped the pastor's head by the hair and threw it so hard that when it hit the officer, it broke every bone in his face. James walked around the squad car where the cop was lying and ripped his throat out.

"So, yeah we were talking about slaves, right? " James continued. "We definitely need some slaves."

***

As of the last census, Defiance County, Ohio had 38,286 residents. In just a day, Evelyn and James had brought the apocalypse to the county. With the help of one of Gertrude's sisters, Ophelia cranked her wheel, and a barrier of hellfire circled the town. The few thousand of Defiance's residents were enslaved and tasked with collecting the bones of the dead. Sadie Mcgowan was one of the slaves. She could be seen hauling an armful of bones across the scorched ground to the spot where they were constructing a ladder.

Jacob's Ladder was the vision of some asshole in the Old Testament. It was essentially a ladder or stairway to heaven. James loved symbology, so what better way to make it to heaven than to build the ladder. Not only build it, but build it from the bones of God's children.

Within a week, the entirety of Ohio was a wasteland. Every other state in the union had declared a state of emergency, but there was nothing they could do to stop the spread of hellfire. The Sisters of Gertrude were all turning their wheels and the apocalypse was upon us. Each person that died was another piece of the ladder that was quickly getting closer to the gates of Heaven.

"I love the work we are doing, but something feels a little off," James said.

"What do you mean?" asked Evelyn.

They were walking side by side through the Southwest Ohio city of Cincinnati. They strolled amongst the fire, along the path that led between the piles of the dead. James was leading his pale horse, Apocalyptica, by the reins behind him.

"Well, when we finally get up to Heaven and confront Grandma, we will need something to kill her."

"What do you mean? We've done fine with our bare hands so far?"

"Yeah, but we are killing *God*, you know? We need something special."

"I swear, James, you and your symbolism shit. It's always making extra work."

"Come on, we are already in Cincinnati. I know a guy down in Kentucky that helped out Jim when he needed some special weaponry."

***

James and Evelyn started their walk across the bridge that led over the Ohio river and into Kentucky. The river now ran less with water and more with blood. As they began to cross the state line, they were confronted by Michael.

The Archangel Michael is credited with defeating Satan during the war in Heaven. He is often depicted as a warrior, carrying a shield and a flaming sword, with his armor shining bright and his angel wings spread wide.  However, that was a long time ago.

Michael still had his sword and shield, but he had his flannel shirt tucked into a pair of Wranglers and wore some dirty, old shit kickin' boots. His gut was starting to sag over his belt, and he looked smaller than you'd expect, especially when he stood in front of his oversized pickup truck.

James and Evelyn stopped at the sight of Michael. Mike, as he now went by, spit some brown liquid on the ground and moved the chew around in his mouth.

"That's far enough, you two. Why don't ya turn around and go on back to Ohio." He pronounced it, *Ohiya.*

"Who the fuck are you?" asked Evelyn.

James leaned towards Eve and said, "I think that's the Archangel, Michael. I mean, I wouldn't know that if he didn't have the sword and shield."

"Yeah, he just looks like some fuckin' hick."

"Hey!" Mike interrupted. "I said turn around. You've come far enough."

"Yeah?" Evelyn responded. "Says who?"

"Says God. I am Michael, The Archangel of Heaven. And Kentucky...well Kentucky is God's country."

"Angel, huh?" asked Evelyn. "If you're an angel, where are your wings?"

"Not that it's any of your business," Michael responded, "but I had Sharky down at the shop cut 'em off. This little girl asked me once if I was a fairy. I ain't no fuckin fairy. Ain't no queers allowed in God's country."

Eve and James looked at each other and James said, "Let's level this fucking place."

Michael put up a valiant effort to save "God's country," but when it was all said and done, he died on his knees, with his own sword stuck through his chest and out his back. He died bent backwards like a rockstar sliding on his knees across the stage, looking to the heavens.

The crows plucked his eyes out and James called more birds over to eat his flesh. Both James and Evelyn felt a rush from absorbing the angel meat. They collected as many of Michael's bones as they could and put them in the horse's saddlebags.

The duo tore through Kentucky even faster than they did in Ohio. The entire state burned while the few survivors banded together into groups, trying to help each other live just a little longer in their new hellscape. Many of the people that remained were covered in boils and sores. Their flesh rotting. Their hair and teeth falling out.

Evelyn and James were riding Apocalyptica when they came to an old house. On the porch sat a man all by himself. He was holding a handgun, and several dead bodies were scattered on what used to be his lawn. They looked to have either been shot or stabbed.

The man sat calmly, either not noticing James and Evelyn, or not caring that they were there. To the right of the man's porch, a portly, naked, and very dead man was greased up and being roasted like a pig over the fire.

"You okay down there, Ned?" the man asked the clearly dead human. "Is it getting too hot for ya? Nah, it looks like you could roast a little longer, bud. But hurry up, I'm getting hungry."

The man reared back and laughed at himself. He had some boils on his face and arms, but other than that, he seemed fine.

Evelyn looked at the man in astonishment. "Is that guy a demon or something? He seems to be doing incredibly well, given that it's the end of the world."

"Nope," answered James. "That's no demon. That's the man we've come to see."

Joshua Ramone was an all-around badass, but a knifemaker by trade. He was a normal human being in the ways of flesh and blood, but no one fucked with Josh. People came from all over the physical world and beyond to get a J.R. blade.

They dismounted the horse and started to walk towards Josh on his porch. Josh didn't even look up when he said, "Y'all can stop right there. That's far enough."

They both stopped and James spoke. “Joshua, we don’t wish you any harm. We are well aware of who you are and what you do. We are in need of a blade.”

“I don’t know if you’ve noticed or not,” Josh responded, “but it’s the end of the fuckin’ world. And I don’t have any blades that I want to give away. I just might need ’em.”

“What if I told you this blade would be used to kill God?”

“Kill God, eh?” Josh finally looked up. “I’m listening. But first, let me get Ned off this roaster. You’re done, aren’t ya Ned? Yeah, you’re ready big man...”

Josh led them to a shed behind his house. Evelyn tried to make some small talk.

“You seem to be doing better than most, considering the circumstances.”

“Yeah, well those dead people on the lawn thought they could come and try to steal my shit. As you can see, that didn’t work out so well for them. I was just trying to survive and mind my own business. I’ve been preparing for the end of the world my entire adult life. It’s not my fault they weren’t prepared.”

“And, uh, what’s the deal with your buddy Ned?” Evelyn asked.

“Ahh he was just an annoying ass next door neighbor. You know, every fall he always blew his leaves into my fucking yard. I figured you have to improvise in times like these, so I thought I’d eat the son of a bitch.”

Evelyn looked at Joshua wide-eyed and thought maybe they could use him on their team. But James interrupted.

"Can you make something out of these?"

"Bones? Sure I can make something gnarly out of some bones."

"These just aren't any bones, Joshua. These are angel bones."

"Ho-ly shit. Really? Fuck yeah, now I'm really inspired."

Josh closed his eyes as he held the bones in his hands. He ran his fingers slowly over them, sensing the form they were meant to take. Once he was satisfied, Josh walked over to a shelf where he had a battery-powered radio with a tape deck. He put in his worn-out copy of *Black Sabbath Vol. 4* and hit the play button. *Wheels of Confusion* blared as Josh gathered his materials and took them to his work station. He flipped on his generator and started up the grinder, but didn't put the bones to the grindstone until *The Straightener* began to play. Once the first note hit, Josh became a different man.

The dust of angel bones filled the air. Sparks that rivaled lightning shot off every time the bones hit the grinder, but Josh never as much as flinched. He wasn't going to stop until his vision had become a reality. It only took him a little over three minutes to fashion the blade that James had planned to use to kill God.

"Here it is. Probably the last blade I'll ever make. I present to you, The Straightener."

The blade, officially named The Straightener, was beautiful and unlike anything anyone had ever seen before. Jagged yet smooth. Heavy yet light. It was everything James had imagined it would be, and so much more.

"What do we owe you?" James asked.

"The only payment I need is that you complete your task and kill that arrogant motherfucker God. That bastard ain't done anything good for anybody."

"That's the plan," James responded. "And just so you know, God is actually a woman."

"No shit? Well, stick this blade straight up her twat then! I don't give a fuck."

James and Evelyn left, and Josh had worked up an appetite. He intended to finish what he started and carve up Ned for supper, but he launched into a coughing fit.

The thing about angel dust is that it is quick to regenerate. Josh didn't wear his mask while grinding, like he normally would have, and he inhaled a hell of a lot of bone dust. His dry cough quickly turned wet and uncontrollable. Blood started spewing from his mouth with each cough, as the bone dust began to grow back into jagged bones that punctured his lungs.

Josh collapsed next to Ned, who was all greased up and ready to eat. Josh never got a taste of his neighbor. With his last breath, Josh struggled to utter his final words. "Fuck you, Ned, and your fucking leaves."

The angel bone punctured Josh's heart and then burst through his chest. It continued to grow and creep along the ground like vines, as Josh lay there dead.

# Chapter Eighteen

# The Fifth Trumpet of Revelation

Mary stood before The Heavenly Board in the conference room. She was as radiant and beautiful as ever.

"You've heard the trumpets. You know what is happening," Mary said to the seven members of the board.

"I will be reinstated, yes?"

Before anyone else could speak, the sound of the fifth trumpet blared, shaking the room they were in. Gary had grabbed the table and let out a whimper when the room shook. They were all scared shitless.

Meredith was sitting to Gary's left. She spoke with a tremble in her voice. "All in favor of reinstating Mary, say aye."

All seven members quickly responded, "Aye."

Mary took her seat at the head of the table.

"What, uh..." Jeremiah stuttered, "what do we do now?"

"We wait."

# Chapter Nineteen

---

# Hole in the Sky

---

Evelyn and James rode Apocalyptica back to Ohio. They arrived just as the stairway to Heaven, built from the bones of God's children, was being completed by their human slaves. They stood at the base of the steps, side by side. Brother and sister. The grandchildren of God and Satan. The spawn of Igor Rotten, who could possibly be the most worthless person to ever live.

Evelyn said, "You know, I've really been digging the theme music thing you've got going on. I thought it was cheesy at first, but now I don't think I want to ascend the stairway to Heaven without a gnarly ass riff."

"Give it a shot," James said. "Let's see what you come up with."

Evelyn closed her eyes and searched for the perfect song. The opening notes of *Stairway to Heaven* by Led Zeppelin began to play.

"Are you fucking kidding me? Could you pick a more obvious song?"

"Ha! I'm just fucking with you. That's not really my pick. How about this?"

*Hole in the Sky* by Black Sabbath started to play.

"Oh HELL yeah!" James exclaimed.

*I'm looking through a hole in the sky*
*I'm seeing nowhere through the eyes of a lie*
*I'm getting closer to the end of the line*
*I'm living easy where the sun doesn't shine*

James had his hand on The Straightener that was sheathed at his side. Without saying another word, Evelyn and James looked at each other, shrugged their shoulders, and took the first steps on the path to Heaven.

*Hole in the sky, take me to heaven*
*Window in time, through it I fly*
*I've seen the stars disappear in the sun*
*The shooting's easy if you've got the right gun*

# Chapter Twenty

# The Sixth Trumpet of Revelation

The sixth trumpet sounded like an air horn during a bombing in the second world war. All of Heaven shook like it was built on a fault line and this was "the big one."

Baby, it WAS the big one.

All the residents had scattered to the furthest edges of Heaven, scared of what was coming. Saint Pete's post had been abandoned, and the souls waiting to be judged were in a panic. They rushed the gates and banged and screamed to be let in, trampling each other in the process.

God sat in a folding chair near the pit that had formed in the center of Heaven, smoking a cigarette. The pit swirled with dark clouds and violent winds. Through the lightning and the rain, she could see the last few steps of the stairway made of bones.

The sixth trumpet finally stopped blaring. Instead, Mary could now hear *Hole in the Sky* by Black Sabbath. It got progressively louder, and suddenly a massive murder of crows began spewing from the pit. They seemed to Mary to be never-ending as they started circling in the heavenly skies above her, dimming the light like the ashes and smoke of a super volcano that just erupted.

Mary was transfixed by the birds and almost didn't notice as her grandchildren, James and Evelyn, emerged from the pit.

James spoke first. "Hello, Grandmother."

Evelyn stood back a little, watching as Mary stood from her chair and flicked her cigarette into the pit. She walked slowly toward James and, as she got closer, James could see the tears welling up in the corner of her eyes.

James hadn't anticipated the feelings he was experiencing, seeing his grandmother for the first time. He had only been imagining her head on a stake, prominently displayed next to him as he sat on his throne as the King of Nothing Left.

Mary got close to James, seemingly unafraid, and embraced him with a hug.

"It's so good to see you," Mary whispered into his ear. "Look at you, more powerful than I had ever imagined."

James stood paralyzed after she let go. Tears began streaming down his face. He had just felt the arms of God hold him, and he didn't know what love felt like until that very moment.

Mary wiped away her own tears and looked at Evelyn, who was still standing by herself; her guard was up with a perplexed look on her face.

"Don't think I've forgotten about you, Evie."

Mary made her way over to Evelyn and wrapped her tightly in her arms. Evelyn began to cry, too. With just a hug, God had seemingly made both James and Evelyn forget they were ever hellbent on her destruction.

Mary grabbed both of them by the hand. She looked at Evelyn, and then at James.

"We have a lot to talk about, don't we?"

"Well, we might as well get everyone else here. If we are going to do this, we should do this right."

There was a flash of white light, and suddenly, the trio became a crowd.

"Well, I don't think that's what Christians had in mind when they came up with the rapture, but I guess that was it," Mary mused.

Kristin, who just a second before, was a monstrous tentacled beast with a gun for a dick ready to eat a baby, was now a monstrous tentacled beast with a gun for a dick, but in Heaven. Jim was mid-scream when the rapture happened, and he took this opportunity to get up and run away from Kristin. He looked around hysterically as he cradled Remi. Everyone was staring at him.

"What the *fuck* happened to you, Jim?" God asked her former lover, Satan.

George and Rosemary made the trip, too. They stood together with their hands over their mouths as they looked at the castrated and mutilated man they knew to be Lucifer, ruler of the underworld.

With all the commotion, no one noticed Igor sitting on the ground near the pit. He stood up and joined the group. They all stood in a circle and looking back and forth at each other.

"Like I was saying before everyone got here, we have a lot to talk abo--"

Eve wasn't listening to Mary's speech. She looked around at the group that had been brought together.

Grandma God gave her a hug and made her feel a love that she had never felt before. She lived a life filled with grief and trauma. She was neglected, abused, and raped. And all God did was let it happen. Was she supposed to just let that slide now?

Her half-brother James came to find her, buy why? He didn't give a shit about her existence before. Was it only because of some vision he had? He knew she was powerful and needed her help. As far as she knew, his intentions were purely selfish.

Satan and James' mom Kristin obviously had their own thing going on over there.

George and Rosemary. She felt like she could have loved George and Rosemary as her own family.

Then there was her dad. Igor was the catalyst for everything awful that had ever happened to her.

# Chapter Twenty-one

# The Seventh Trumpet of Revelation

The group stood around Mary, captivated by her beauty and enraptured with her speech. But before Mary could finish her next thought, the seventh trumpet sounded. It was the loudest of them all, bringing everyone to their knees with their hands over their ears. Everyone except Mary.

Mary had stopped talking. The Straightener protruded through the front of her neck. She gargled and gagged on the blood that poured from her mouth.

James looked down and noticed that his blade was gone. When he looked back up, Evelyn was standing where Mary had been. She held God's head in her hands by the hair, similar to way she held the head of the pedophile pastor. Evelyn lifted Mary's head up high and let the blood from God's neck pour into her mouth. It trickled down the front of her chin and her shirt.

The group looked at Evelyn with absolute horror and confusion. Behind them, the pit began to rage with bubbling lava and hellfire.

Evelyn looked at the group and simply stated, “No one survives.”

## Chapter Twenty-two

# No One Survives – Part III

George and Rosemary were good people, tasked only with reincarnating Igor Rotten and then his daughter, Evelyn. Their hearts were pure. They loved Igor and they loved Evelyn. Eve showed her ruthlessness by killing them first. She plunged The Straightener into Rosemary's chest. When she pulled the blade back out, she brought Rosemary's heart with it. George screamed, "Nooo!" as Rosemary turned to him, to look in his eyes one more time.

Evelyn took a bite of Rosemary's heart and it splattered on George's face. She jammed The Straightener through one of his eyes, then the other. George screamed again and fell to his knees, and Eve slit his throat. She grabbed both of their bodies and threw them nonchalantly into the boiling pit.

Kristin knew Evelyn was coming for her next and made the first move, but it was no use. Evelyn had just murdered God and drank her blood. She was now nearly unstoppable. Evelyn used The

Straightener to sever each of her tentacles. Blood squirted from where her limbs used to be, and her mannequin face gasped as she fell to the ground. Evelyn ripped the dick gun from Kristin's crotch, and the tearing skin sounded like wet velcro being pulled apart . Evelyn turned the gun around and unloaded the clip into Kristen's stupid plastic face.

Into the pit!

Jim had been broken beyond repair. He was a shell of his former greatness and dropped to his knees, begging Evelyn to spare him. She bent forward and pressed her forehead firmly up against her grandfather's and said, "Fuck you." She grabbed Remi from his arms and bit her in the neck. She held her up, much like she did Mary's head, and simultaneously consumed and bathed in the ass baby's blood. She tossed Remi aside like nothing more than trash.

Into the piiiiiit!

Jim cried out with a sort of agony that only a parent could understand. Eve thought about letting him live, because all he wanted to do was die. But it was a fleeting thought and she pushed The Straightener into his gut, not once, not twice, but three times and then...

TOSSED HIM INTO THE PIT!

She came to Igor, her father. He sat by, like he had always done, and watched the horrible events unfold.

"Evie," he stuttered. "Evie, it doesn't have to be like this."

"Don't call me that."

Evelyn stuck The Straightener into Igor's chest, just above his neck. She gutted him all the way down to the bottom of his abdomen, splitting him wide open. She put the blade down, took both hands, and ripped his torso into two pieces.

As Igor died, he didn't see his daughter murdering him. He didn't even feel it. He imagined spinning around in circles, with little Evie hanging from his arm. In his head, he sang the song that he would sing to her just before he tucked her in to bed.

*Evie, the moon is out tonight*
*Evie, the stars are shining bright*
*Evie, it's time to close your eyes*
*Evie, it's time to say goodnight*

Eve couldn't have cared less about Igor's feelings. She had a handful of her father's insides and took a few bites before tossing both pieces of him...

INTO THE MOTHERFUCKING PIT!

James didn't know what to think. His crows still circled above as he watched Evelyn's bloody massacre. The hug he had gotten from Mary had changed something in him, and he wished Evelyn hadn't done what she had just done. He wanted closure. He wanted to know love. He wanted more than death.

James approached Evelyn.

"I don't know what I expected, but it wasn't this."

"Well thanks for the help," Evelyn replied sarcastically.

"Sorry, I just thought maybe we'd do a little more talking first. Maybe get some answers about our family."

Evelyn took The Straightener and plunged it into Jamie Rotten's heart. He looked down at the blade in his chest, her hand still clutching the hilt. She grabbed Jamie's throat with her other hand and squeezed as she pushed him backward to the edge of the pit.

He waited for Evelyn to say something profound before she tossed him into the pit, but she just smirked and rolled her eyes. She left The Straightener in his chest, took two steps back, and then front kicked the butt of the knife, driving the blade as far as it could go into James's chest. He fell backward...

Into the pit.

# Chapter Twenty-three

# Brand New God

Evelyn kicked in the door of the boardroom where the seven members of the Heavenly board had been hiding. She took the seat at the head of the table, leaned back, and put her feet up. She licked some of the blood from her fingers.

“There are going to be some changes around here. You. Yeah, you. You look like you think you’re important. ”

Gary gulped, and the sound he made was the loudest sound in the room.

“Be a gentleman and show me to my new room.”

***

Evelyn walked through the room Mary used to occupy. She stood in front of the wall of monitors and watched the chaos that was transpiring on Earth. Evelyn and James may have started the

Apocalypse in Ohio, but the rest of the world was finishing the job.

The panic they induced caused tensions that spread to all the other countries in the world. It didn't take long for the super powers of Earth to start measuring their dick sizes by threatening nuclear war. It seemed Earth was on the brink of World War III, and there was no stopping it.

Curiosity got the best of Evelyn. She wondered to herself how these monitors actually worked. She noticed a group of cables banded together, disappearing into the wall. She went to the wall and knocked on it. The hollow echo told her there was space behind the wall.

"Gary! Get the fuck in here!"

Gary rushed in to the room. "Yes, my Lord?"

"Eww, gross. Don't call me that. I don't know what I want to be called yet, but it's not that. That's some weird *Game of Thrones* bullshit."

"Yes, uh...ma'am?"

"Whatever, it doesn't matter. At least not for you."

Gary didn't understand, and the look on his face expressed just that. It was the last expression he ever made as Evelyn back handed him across the face so hard that it knocked his head off his shoulders. His body stood headless for a few moments before it fell to the ground and blood poured from his neck.

Evelyn picked up his head and used it as a hammer to make a hole in the wall. While she bashed the severed head against the drywall, she realized that she was powerful enough to just bust through. She turned Gary's smashed head so they were face to face.

"Sorry, Gary. I may have been a little overzealous with the decapitation. But, to be fair, I can't imagine you being any more useful than you are right now."

Evelyn chucked Gary's head behind her and finished breaking through the wall. What she found on the other side was more than just a room. It looked to be an entire floor of a hospital. The cables connected to the monitors ran down a hallway straight ahead of her. She picked up the cables and let them run through her hand, leading her down the path.

Evelyn's walk was longer than she expected it to be, and quite boring. There didn't seem to be anyone around, and the place was dull and sterile. It was mostly dark, with patches of fluorescent lights that flickered like they were ready to burn out at any moment. She was about to give up when she saw a privacy curtain up ahead. The cables led directly underneath it.

When she got to the curtain, she didn't hesitate to slide it open. She didn't know what she expected to see, but it wasn't the elderly woman lying in front of her.

It was obvious that this woman was incredibly old, but she was alive. She was on life support, with a machine mimicking steady breaths that she couldn't take herself. The top of her skull was missing; it was sawed off with surgical precision. The cables were plugged directly into the woman's brain.

Evelyn stood over the woman, unsure what to do with her discovery. Her curiosity burning hotter than ever, she looked through the cabinets and found the surgical tools that had been used to remove the top of the unknown woman's skull.

Evelyn sat down in a chair next to the bed with the medical drill she found. She pressed the drill bit to her temple and began to drill a hole into her own skull. It was painful, and she screamed as the drill first pierced her skin, throwing blood around the room and onto the comatose old lady. She had to push harder to get through her skull, but was careful to stop as soon as she felt the resistance give way. She didn't want to pierce her brain. Removing the drill bit from her head, she undid one of the cables from the old woman's brain, and plugged it into her own.

Eve's body went limp, and her consciousness was transported from her mind. Suddenly, she was no longer just Eve, she was *everything*. She was the universe. She was all of the worlds within it. She was every life, every death, every atom in every bit of matter. And she was helpless.

She shared this consciousness with the old woman, who was pleased to have some company.

"Have you ever planted marigolds in your garden? I always planted marigolds because they were easy to grow. They made me feel like I was good at something. Like I could actually keep things alive."

Evelyn just listened as the woman went on her diatribe about flowers without even as much as an introduction. She supposed the woman hadn't had a visitor in a very long time. She was probably insane.

"The problem with marigolds, though, is that they spread like fuckin' wild fire. Sometimes, you have to dig them up to keep them from taking over the whole garden. And when I would dig up the pesky runaways, I'd always come across some slugs. Those gross, slimy, little land mollusks love to live underneath marigolds."

"I would think to myself, what the hell is the point of a slug? It's a pest that doesn't do anything good for anybody. I'd get so mad about these worthless creatures that I'd go inside and get a can of salt. I'd take joy in shaking the salt all over those little bastards and watch them melt right in front of my eyes. Hell, I got to the point where I liked finding them, just so I could salt the fuckers."

"Then, one day, I ended up here. I don't know how, but I became the universe. I became everything. You know that, don't you? You are here now. You can feel it. You are *it.*"

"It took me a long time to realize it, but once I did, I only wished to be able to tell this story and have someone listen. Take a look at this vessel we are in right now. Take a look at the vessel that contains the entire universe, literally everything that we have ever known to exist."

Evelyn didn't know how she did it, but she looked at the vessel that held her and everything together inside of it. The universe was contained inside of a slug.

The old woman cackled, "Can you believe this shit? Everything that has ever happened is absolutely meaningless. Everyone that has ever lived or died was for no reason at all! The heroes, the villains, the love, and the hatred. The buildings erected, torn down, and erected again were all for naught. The progress of mankind was only progressing towards this, right now. We are all just one big slimy piece of slug shit."

Evelyn didn't know what to say. This meant even her quest to be God was meaningless. Her epic conquest was, in the end, meant to be nothing but slug shit.

"And now for the best part. Look what lies ahead. We are almost there."

Evelyn felt a slight burning against her skin as small, white asteroid like fragments pelted her. Only a few at first, but then more frequently. The slug was floating towards a swirling white hole. It was headed straight for The Salt.

"This slug is going to meet its demise, just like all those slugs that ate up my marigolds." The woman laughed again. This time she couldn't stop.

Evelyn was scared she wasn't going to be able to get out, and that she would be dissolved in The Salt with the crazy slug lady. But she woke up and was back in Heaven's hospital, sitting next to the old woman on life support. A nurse stood in front of her with the cable in her hand. She had pulled it out of Evelyn's head.

"What are you doing? You can't be here!"

Eve sat in the chair, ignoring the angry nurse as she babbled on. She was ruminating on what she had just experienced. The entire universe was just a slug on a crash course with a salty death. She felt it. She knew it was true.

She stood up and broke the neck of the nurse without as much as a second glance. Then she looked at the woman who clearly should have died long ago. She followed the power cord of the machine that was breathing for the old slug lady all the way to the outlet in the wall.

Eve put her hand on the end of the plug, took a deep breath, and said, " Fuck it. No one survives."

Then she pulled the plug.

***

If you are old enough to have grown up with television that went "off the air" at night, you'll know what I'm talking about when I say "static snow." When Evelyn pulled that plug, she pulled the plug on everything. Reality and beyond went "off air." All that was left was the "static snow," and the white noise it creates.

The slug plunged into the white hole known as The Salt, and now we are all gone. All of us except Igor.

Igor, the anomaly of the slugverse, was destined to survive, forevermore. Even where there is nothing, there is still Igor. He found himself back in his old movie theatre with his buddy Todd. He was strapped in his chair, with his eyes held open, being forced to watch every miserable moment he ever experienced. At least he had a few new films to watch this time around.

To Be Continued in Survivor (Rotten: Book 3)

Due to be released May 16, 2022

# Afterword

Thank you for reading No One Survives (Rotten: Book 2.) I hope you enjoyed it! As an independent and self published author, online reviews mean absolutely everything. They are essential to the visibility and continued success of each self published book and independent author.

That being said, I am asking that you go to Amazon or Goodreads and give Rotten the rating and review you think it deserves.

Thank you again for reading my book. I hope to see you at the end of the next one!

Most Sincerely,

Buzz Parcher

Made in the USA
Monee, IL
16 May 2022